It didn't matter that Nush had spent a decade working for and with Caio.

That they'd been business partners since her eighteenth birthday. With her grandfather's encouragement, she'd entered a partnership with Caio to build a subcompany based on the software model she'd built. His knowledge of the market and his risk-taking meant she'd made millions before she'd turned twenty-one.

It didn't matter that her acne had cleared up, that she had filled out enough to have a semblance of curves to go with her arms and legs or that, in the last year, she'd dated men ranging from models to CEOs to even a congressman in a desperate bid to rid herself of this strange fascination.

It didn't matter how much she'd changed or who she became. When it came to Caio, she was still that awed fourteen-year-old who couldn't help but stare. He was still the tall, dark Brazilian god who made her skin flush, her heart flutter, her breath do wonky things with one simple look. The only saving grace was that she'd never betrayed herself or the extent of her...desire for him.

Billion-Dollar Fairy Tales

Once upon a temptation...

Meet the Reddy sisters—Nush, Mira and Yana. As the granddaughters of tech tycoon Rao Reddy, their lives have been full of glitz and glamour. Until tragedy strikes and their beloved grandfather passes away. Amid their devastation, each girl finds a note, Rao's last gift for them to help them live out their dreams. But chasing their happiness won't be a smooth ride!

Nush has been in love with her longtime family friend and billionaire boss, Caio, for longer than she can remember. She's ready to move on... but then he proposes they have a convenient marriage!

Read Nush and Caio's story in
Marriage Bargain with Her Brazilian Boss

Available now!

Look out for Mira's and Yana's stories, both coming soon!

Tara Pammi

MARRIAGE BARGAIN WITH HER BRAZILIAN BOSS

HARLEQUIN®
PRESENTS™

Recycling programs
for this product may
not exist in your area.

ISBN-13: 978-1-335-58413-7

Marriage Bargain with Her Brazilian Boss

Copyright © 2023 by Tara Pammi

For questions and comments about the quality of this book,
please contact us at CustomerService@Harlequin.com.

Harlequin Enterprises ULC
22 Adelaide St. West, 41st Floor
Toronto, Ontario M5H 4E3, Canada
www.Harlequin.com

Printed in U.S.A.

got about small things. Like stocking groceries and buying clothes and books for Nush, like making sure she spent time outside and with kids her own age.

Even with an unconventional mother who'd told her at the age of eight that she'd been borne out of an affair, Nush had always longed for a permanent home base, a close-knit family. Especially the one her half-sisters had with her paternal grandparents in California, the one she'd got her first glimpse of at the same age. Their father—a has-been artist and a raging alcoholic—apparently liked variety in his lovers, and so she, Yana and her oldest sister, Mira, all had different mothers.

As allergic as Mama was to the institution of marriage, she'd never denied Anushka the knowledge of her father's family. The six summers Nush had spent with her grandparents and her two half-sisters at their sprawling estate in California had soon become the highlight of those year.

And now she would be back with them for another summer. At least that's what Mama had told Nush in between tears, all the while issuing conditions and threats and warnings about her well-being to the man who represented Nush's grandparents. All of which had been received with a patience and equanimity and even a kind-

PROLOGUE

ANUSHKA REDDY LOOKED around the luxurious cabin of the private jet, but it was hard, as a four-teen-year-old, to maintain interest in the aircraft or anything else for that matter when excitement filled her belly with a thousand swarming but-terflies.

To stay with her grandparents and her half-sisters, for the entire summer.

Instant guilt speared through her at the thought. It wasn't that she didn't love her mom and all the adventures she had with her. As a world-renowned environmental activist and an artist, her mom traveled all over the world—sometimes to showcase her work, most times in search of inspiration—which meant Nush had, in her fourteen years, lived in the most interest-ing places in the world.

But her mom was also absentminded and mer-curial and prone to long periods of melancholy and depression. And when that low hit, she forness that she hadn't associated with… *Caio Oliveira.* And yet he'd been infinitely gentle with Mama's irrational outbursts.

Nush pushed her thick glasses up the bridge of her nose and studied him with as much covertness as she was capable of.

Caio was a constant in her grandparents' life. A larger-than-life former soccer player slash current coding genius from Brazil that her grandfather considered his right-hand man. She'd only ever glanced at him while hiding behind Mira because one only ever looked at the sun from a distance.

But now, at such close quarters, Nush revised her opinion of him. He wasn't the sun. He was tall, broad, a dark golden-skinned god from one of the mythical universes that populated her favorite role-playing video game. Light brown eyes with golden flecks shone with a wicked intelligence, hooded under thick dark brows that seemed to see toc much with jet-black wavy hair that was cut close to his head and a jawline that was usually found on male models in fashion magazines. The man was too…*virile*, she thought, testing the word she'd heard Yana use once.

If they were animals, Caio would be the alpha at the top.

There was no other way to describe him, especially when she was a bespectacled, acne-ridden, gangly teenager who didn't know what to do with her legs or arms or her suddenly overactive hormones.

It was new to her—this sudden influx of *feelings* she had no control over. Usually, her logical brain was her best friend. The thing she could rely on to keep her strong when Mama wasn't, which had been a lot in the last two years.

But she couldn't just keep staring at him for the rest of the flight. The last thing she wanted him to think was that she was still a little weird and nerdy.

"Why didn't Thaata come to pick me up?" she said, once the flight attendant, who'd been making eyes at him, had left them alone. She wasn't as fluent in the language her father's family spoke as Mira was but she was determined to make a real effort to learn this summer.

A smile lifted one corner of his mouth, drawing a dimple on one side. "So you do talk."

An overwhelming rush of shyness hit Nush like a tidal wave. She could feel her cheeks reddening. Probably the tip of her nose too. "Of course I talk, Mr. Oliveira. But only when there's something important to be said." She cringed and sighed. Why couldn't she sound normal for once?

"Now, that's an admirable quality I find rarely,

especially among adults. And no Mr. Oliveira business, Anushka. It makes me feel old."

"You *are* old," Nush blurted out, fighting the floaty sensation in her belly at how good her name sounded on his lips.

Laughter burst from him, loud and deep, drawing crinkles around his mouth and eyes. Her lungs felt like they did when she'd gone deep-sea diving—gasping for breath, unable to comprehend the magnificent beauty that surrounded her.

His smile took him from handsome to gorgeous, with a stopover at stunning.

"I mean…you're quite a lot older than me," she said, wanting to hide under the table between them.

"Twenty-seven is not that old, minx. But I'm jaded and cynical, so…" A shadow crossed his eyes, gone in an instant. "Also, the title of Mr. Oliveira belonged to my father. I'd feel like a cheap fake if I used that."

A glimmer of raw ache made those eyes flash golden at the mention of his father. "If you want me to say your name right, you better teach me it," she said, immediately wanting to distract him. "I know it doesn't rhyme with *mayo*."

"Cristo, no," he said with a mock shudder. Planting his forearms on the table, he leaned forward. "It's Caio," he said slowly.

Nush repeated his name, a few times too many even after she got it, loving the sound of it on her lips.

"Perfect, Princesa."

Mouth falling open, she bristled. "Why do you call me Princess?"

"Isn't that what your grandpa calls you? Why is that?"

"Promise you won't laugh at me."

"I wouldn't dare."

"I was always too fond of fairy tales."

"Why would I laugh at that?"

"Mama used to tell me that life's too important to bury my head in outdated tales."

He opened his mouth and then closed it. And Nush knew he'd swallowed away his own cynical opinion so that he didn't corrupt hers. That little, innate kindness instantly made her like him a little more. Now she could say she liked Caio for more than his looks.

"What do you like about them?" he asked with a genuine tone.

"That there's always a happy ending, whatever the affliction the princesses have. That there's always someone right for them. It doesn't matter if they're too quiet, or shy or even strange. I do agree that some of them feel outdated but then I just rewrite them in my head the way I want them."

"As long as you don't forget that real life doesn't work like that, Princesa. Sometimes, there's no happy ending. There's only crushing disappointment, dealt both by circumstance and people. Love is sometimes not enough."

"That's your opinion," she said, tilting her chin up.

He shrugged and the gesture pulled her attention to the breadth of his shoulders. "I never answered your question, did I? Your grandfather wanted to come, as did Mira and Yana," he said, mentioning her sisters. "But your grandmother had an asthma episode recently, and as I was making this trip anyway," he said softly, "I offered to pick you up."

"Is Nanamma okay now?"

"She is."

"Are you and Yana still dating?" Nush wanted to disappear the moment she heard her question.

Caio was her first official crush and she was already finding this whole thing painful. Not for a second could she betray her thoughts. Not especially now, when she was moving to California and would see him on a regular basis.

Not that she'd been able to stop thinking of him and Yana since she'd realized their visitor was Caio. She adored both her sisters. To see him with Yana—who was so stunningly gorgeous that, at nineteen, she was already highly sought after as a model—would've felt awkward and weird. There was that word again.

She stole a look from under her lashes, and was relieved that he didn't look irritated. "Sorry, it's none of my business," she whispered.

"It's okay, Princesa. Honest curiosity never bothers me." He drummed his fingers on the table between them. "Yana and I are not dating anymore. We realized it would hurt your grandparents and Mira and now you immensely, if we killed each other as a result of all that proximity. Which turned to be a distinct possibility."

Nush burst out laughing. It had been clear, even to her, that they really weren't suited to each other. She instantly sobered up as another worrying thought struck. "You and Yana are still friends now that you've broken up, right?"

"And why does the thought that we might not be put such a frown here, Anushka?" he said, pointing a finger at her forehead.

She pushed the glasses up the bridge of her slightly too large nose. "I don't want to have to take sides, that's all."

His thick brows drawing together, he looked thunderstruck. "Take sides? How do you come to that, Princesa?"

"I know how much Thaata values you. As high-maintenance as Yana can be—that's what Nanamma says about her—I wouldn't want to be caught between you two when I finally have a full family."

The shock in his eyes deepened until slowly, another smile warmed them and they glowed brightly. "I see why your grandfather thinks you're precious."

Heat swarmed Nush's cheeks. Damn it, why had she opened her mouth at all? "It's not like I like you like you...that would just be ewww... because you're like really old," she added, with extra affectation she'd seen in teen movies.

His raucous laughter enveloped her. The man was really beautiful and his presence did things to her insides—specifically her lower belly and lower, where she'd never felt such things before. Intellectually, she knew what it was but still, it threw her, this feverish fascination. And it scared her a bit too.

"I appreciate your consideration, Princesa. And your generosity in considering me family." His gaze gentled. "Are you looking forward to the summer?"

She smiled. "I've always wanted to be part of a big family. Living with Mama is an adventure but it can also get very lonely." She swallowed at the sudden ache that lodged in her throat. "She was very upset today. Sometimes, she can't help herself. Please don't be angry at her for that."

He tapped at her tightly laced fingers and

shook his head. "Not at all, Anushka. She was upset, yes, but I have enough sense to know that it was her grief at having to send you away." His tone was so gentle that it made the ache turn into a hard lump. "Your mother's a very strong woman to make such hard choices for your well-being. All I took from her reaction today is that she loves you very much. Not every mother could do what she did."

Tears threatened at his kind words and Nush blinked them back. "Do you think it's wrong that I'm so excited about being with Mira and Yana?"

"Not at all." His brow furrowed and his voice deepened. "Never think that. You can be sad and excited at the same time. One doesn't invalidate the other. And families are complicated, *sim*?"

Something in his gaze made her ask, "What about you, Caio? Do you have a big family?"

"Not really. Not anymore at least"

There was a note in his voice that clearly said it wasn't a topic he wanted to talk about. So even as curiosity pricked, she followed his lead and let it be. She didn't want to hurt him by probing into painful matters. Running her hands over the buttery soft leather of her seat, she asked, "So this jet…it's yours, right?"

His eyes twinkled as if he found her endlessly fascinating. "How do you know it's not your grandfather's?"

"My grandparents are immigrants who came to the US with nothing. They'd never waste money on such extravagant luxuries."

"I thought I'd successfully avoided the environmentalist's notice. But I see I didn't escape her smart daughter."

"Mama would have roasted you alive with at least an hour's lecture," Nush said with a laugh. "Is this your present to yourself for soaring stock? You're a millionaire now, aren't you?"

"You're business savvy too? No wonder your grandfather is so excited to have you come live with them."

Nush blushed. "I follow the company news. I invested the allowance Thaata gave me in your stock."

Surprise made him chuckle. "You're an unending delight, Anushka."

"My friends call me Nush," she said, even though she didn't actually have any real-life friends. Only online ones, kids who didn't judge her because online she could pretend that she was perfect. "Plus I'm interested in the finance software you develop. I've been following its development since Thaata and you were discussing it that first time I met you. I'm a coder too."

"Yeah?"

Something about the challenge in his gaze spurred Nush to reach for her backpack. It had been a gift from Mira and Yana on her last visit and it was her favorite possession. Soon, she had the program she'd written open on her laptop. Turning the screen toward him, she rested her chin on her clasped hands and waited for his assessment.

His golden eyes moved over the screen rapidly, and she took the chance to study him to her heart's content, storing away the smallest details.

After several minutes, Caio plopped the laptop closed and whistled.

"You wrote the program?"

She nodded, catching the light of curiosity in his eyes. It was a look she'd seen in her own eyes when she made forward progress.

"How long did it take?"

"A week."

Caio stared at her, his gaze calculating and shrewd. A thrill shot through her when he stuck out a hand between them. Nush let his big hand envelop hers and that swarm of butterflies took flight in her belly again. "What's…this for?"

"A partnership, Princesa. You and I are going to rule the world together."

Nush gave him her hand and promised herself she'd find a boy exactly like Caio when she grew up to fall in love with.

Maybe not as good-looking and magnetic and charming and so…out of her sphere.

But someone like him, nevertheless.

CHAPTER ONE

Nine years later

Step out of your fairy tales, Princess.
Life is to be lived, not read about.

NUSH OPENED AND folded the crisp note that had been delivered to her this morning, two days after Thaata had drawn his last breath. She'd read his handwritten message a thousand times already.

It felt like a sign. More than a sign—a wakeup call.

Had Thaata known how frustrated and unhappy she'd been of late? How stuck she felt? How she was so full of longing and resentment against one man who took up all her waking thoughts?

Her grandfather had taken a turn for the worse in the month since they'd lost their grandmother. It was a shock Nush wasn't sure she or her sisters would recover from soon. A fresh wave of grief made the back of her eyes prickle. Thaata seemed to have known all three of them needed a little more from him. More than the love and acceptance and affection he'd always given them.

Standing against the far wall, she studied the crowd that had gathered in the high-ceilinged living room of their grandparents' colonial-style house to pay their final respects to a man who'd touched so many lives through the tech giant OneTech he'd started two decades ago and that had flourished into a multibillion-dollar company with Caio at the helm in the last decade.

Among the guests were Yana's mother and her stepfather and her stepbrothers. And her older sister Mira's husband, Aristos, even though he and Mira had been separated for the last nine months. Only Mama was absent.

Nush had tried to tell her mother on her last visit to the nursing home that Thaata had taken a turn for the worse, but in the tail end of one of her bad episodes, Mama had only stared back with a glassy look.

Mira had flown in from Greece at a second's notice to look after her grandmother after her heart attack eight months ago and never returned. Not a year ago, her steady, sensible sister had shocked them all by marrying Greek business tycoon Aristos in Las Vegas. They'd never seen Mira so happy. And yet when Yana and Nush had probed Mira about not returning to Aristos, their older sister had burst into tears.

Unsurprisingly now, it was Mira and Caio who effortlessly slipped into the role of playing hosts.

Caio was the true heir to her grandfather's legacy and his vision. Her grandparents had brought up Mira since she'd been a toddler. Ever since her mother had walked out and their father had continued on with his womanizing.

Nush frowned at how good they looked together. Her brother-in-law Aristos's gaze mirrored the same irritation. Which was ridiculous because neither of her sisters were aware that her harmless crush had matured into something else even as Caio dated and discarded more women than Yana did designer handbags.

As if she'd called out his name, Caio flicked a gaze across the room.

Dressed in relentless black, he was like a dark sun among a sea of overly bright stars, all orbiting him constantly for attention. Still searching, he bent from his considerable height to kiss her sister's cheek and walked into the room.

He was looking for her. Nush knew it as surely as her heart fluttered like the mad hare racing off to the finish line. They hadn't talked since their nightlong vigil at Thaata's bedside two nights ago.

Her eyes tracked him across the large living room, caressing his features as eagerly as the sunlight slanting through the high windows did. The high forehead, the deep-set light brown eyes with their golden flecks, the arrogant nose and the thin slash of his mouth were as familiar to her as her own face.

If he'd been stunning when he'd been twenty-seven, almost a decade later now, there was a compelling quality to him that sang to her. A confidence that made clowns of twentysomething men that employed mind games and power plays in the name of dating.

Was it the mantle of responsibility that he wore so well? The well-honed instinct for success? Or the deep-seated streaks of honor and integrity that he suppressed in the boardroom as if they were a weakness but still colored his actions anyway?

It didn't matter that she'd spent the decade working for and with Caio. That they'd been business partners since her eighteenth birthday. With her grandfather's encouragement, she'd entered a partnership with Caio to build a sub-company based on the software model she'd developed. His knowledge of the market, his risk-taking meant she'd made millions before she'd turned twenty-one.

It didn't matter that her acne had cleared up,

that she had filled out enough to have a semblance of curves to go with her arms and legs, or that, in the last year, she'd dated men ranging from models to CEOs to even a congressman in a desperate bid to rid herself of this strange fascination.

It didn't matter how she much she'd changed or who she became. When it came to Caio, she was still that awed fourteen-year-old who couldn't help but stare. He was still the tall, dark Brazilian god that made her skin flush, her heart flutter, her breath do wonky things with one simple look. Somehow the blasted man had imprinted on her sexuality and she needed to do something about it if she didn't want to be sixty and still salivating over him from a distance. The only saving grace was that she'd never betrayed herself or the extent of her...desire for him.

Friends and business partners and shareholders stopped Caio to offer respects, to keep themselves in his good graces. A couple of well-dressed women laid manicured fingers on his forearm. Wordlessly offering to soothe his grief, she thought bitchily.

A wave of relief flooded through her when Caio didn't even flick a look in their direction. Followed by the prickly heat of shame. At least those women had the guts to show him their interest, to make a play for him.

Not like her. Spinning fantasies around him while standing still for years.

Caio's roving gaze stopped when it found her standing under the shadow of a raised beam. The gaunt tightness of his features loosened. Even across the distance, she could see the gentling of the ruthless curve of his mouth. The warmth that deepened the golden flecks of his eyes.

The *I'm here* look that she knew, without doubt, she was the sole recipient of in the entire world. The look that had always made her feel as if there was a special bond between them. Only she got to see this softer, less ruthless version of Caio. The real man that he was under the brilliant, ruthless entrepreneur he showed the world.

But for the first time in nine years, Nush hated it. Hated how she'd boxed herself into this place with him. Hated how it had become a prison that she couldn't break out of.

"If you're going to make a move, do it soon."

Nush jerked her gaze away from Caio to find her sister Yana watching her. While Nush looked like a crow in an unrelenting, sleeveless black T-shirt and black leggings, Yana looked just as inappropriate in neon-pink pants with matching spaghetti top and an oversized jacket with bright white sequins all over it.

Neither of them had wanted to be here. Had

protested about putting on a show of their grief for a loss they wouldn't be over for a long time. But Mira, ever the responsible one, had reminded them that their grandparents would want them there. Would want them to give people who'd loved them just as much a chance to show their respect.

Heat prickled her cheeks as Nush pushed her glasses up her nose. "What…do you mean?"

"It's a wonder he hasn't caught on with how you look at him, Nushie… I mean Caio's not stupid when it comes to women." Yana frowned, her voice pitched thankfully low. "But I guess you both do spend hours attached at the hip and he knows what an introvert you are and that you don't have any real-life friends so maybe he thinks it's normal for you to be fascinated by him."

Nush glared at her sister. "Not everyone is as confident when it comes to sex and romance and affairs as you are."

"I'd never make fun of you." Yana laced her fingers around Nush's stiff ones and squeezed. "I mean, everyone thinks I'm just beauty and no brains and I drove Thaata and Nanamma wild with my antics, and it's kinda true but I'm not completely without substance, Nush."

"Mira and I've never thought that of you," Nush said, feeling angry on her sister's behalf.

Angry at a world that always found fault with women.

Yana was beautiful. Like world-class beautiful, with cheekbones one could sharpen their knives on, a wide, plump mouth that regularly spawned poems and dirty lyrics in homage from fans, a naturally voluptuous figure that had designers and photographers clamoring to showcase their designs. And yet Yana was routinely called a shallow diva by the press, her worth frequently reduced to her looks by her mother. Not that Yana didn't give them all enough fodder by forever getting into one mess or the other.

Beneath it all, Yana hid a heart of gold. It just needed a lot of excavation first. Both her sisters had welcomed her into their lives with open arms, and unconditional love. Nush couldn't imagine getting through the last few years of dealing with her mother's worsening mental health issues without her sisters and Caio.

And just like that, every road in her life wound back to him.

Folding and refolding a note in her hands, Yana gave a tremulous smile. "Thanks, Nushie."

What message had Thaata left for Yana? And Mira, for that matter? Were they feeling as raw and stuck in their lives as she did in her own?

"I wasn't teasing about making your move fast," Yana said softly.

Nush tried for denial but gave up as something in Yana's tone tugged at her. "Why do you say that?"

"You know how Thaata thought you and Peter Huntington Jr. would be a good match and it went to hell because he called you a giraffe with an oversized brain?"

Nush sighed. "I don't need a reminder."

Yana giggled. "It's funny because I think he's an overgrown dinosaur with a pea-sized brain. It's common knowledge Thaata and Peter Sr. have been increasingly at odds since Thaata brought in Caio."

"That was fourteen years ago and without Caio, the company would've never grown as it has."

"I agree. And then Caio roped you in and OneTech grew beyond everyone's expectations. That's one reason Peter Sr. was pushing his son at you. You're the golden goose for OneTech and he wanted to break up you and Caio."

"I'd never work for someone who thinks Caio's the enemy."

"But Peter Sr. doesn't know that and he's a master strategist. Since you and his son went nowhere, talk now is that Laura Huntington and Caio could be the new partnership that could balance out the power struggle."

Nush's heart gave a painful thud. Laura Huntington was everything Nush wasn't. Sophisticated, beautiful, curvy, witty and not at all socially awkward—a perfect counterpart to smooth out Caio's brittle edges. She cleared her throat, trying to budge her heart, which seemed to have lodged itself in her throat. "I thought the Huntingtons hated Caio."

"Not if they get him for a son-in-law. I hate to give her credit but Laura's the total package."

Despite the ever-tightening knot in her belly, Nush laughed. "Why do you hate to give her credit?"

"Huh? How are you so smart in some things and so naive in others, Nushie-kins?" Yana laced her arm through Nush's. "Because she's direct competition for my little sister. On that principle alone, I have to hate her. Also the fact that Laura's an intellectual snob who's always looked down on me might have something to do with it."

On a sudden impulse, Nush wrapped her arms around Yana's waist and planted a hard kiss on her cheek. Her sister stayed stiff at first but slowly relented. Nush bit back tears that felt like they were never far these days.

"We have each other. Always," Yana said, tone full of emotion that she rarely let even her sisters see.

Her grandparents were gone, Mama didn't

want to talk to her most weeks, and now Caio might be making new alliances that would only make her an outsider in his life...it felt like her world would never stop rocking. But she'd always have Mira and Yana, Nush reminded herself, breathing the floral scent of Yana's perfume deep into her lungs. For all that her father had never actually parented her for a single day in her life, he'd given her two wonderful sisters. Nush could forgive him a lot for that.

Yana dabbed at her cheek with a grimace. "I don't see a good reason for Caio to say no to this partnership, Nushie. Laura's brains and beauty and a steadying influence over her father. And we all know Caio will do anything to keep control of OneTech."

Nush couldn't contest the point.

Caio's loyalty to her grandparents was only rivaled by his ambition. More acquisitions, more mergers, more innovation...he'd been on a warpath the last year. While she mostly tuned out those meetings, Nush remembered even her grandfather asking Caio what would be enough and Caio laughing that not until he had something in his hand.

Over the years, Nush had tried to understand where his ambition stemmed from, why no amount of success or wealth was enough for him, but she'd got nowhere. Which had made her realize now how ruthless his personal boundaries were. Yes, she had a familiarity with Caio, more than others had, but she couldn't delude herself that she knew all of him either.

And maybe that's where your fascination comes from, a voice whispered inside her head. For all that he knew every inch of her life, Caio was still a mystery to her. And as a woman who built complex systems that ran some of the biggest infrastructures in the world, it was no wonder she was obsessed with peeling back the layers of what made him want a woman.

As if to prove Yana's point, Laura Huntington ended up being the woman who did halt Caio's purposeful stride toward Nush. Her fingers clutching his, Laura said something to him. Bending down to accommodate Laura's petite frame, long fingers on her shoulder, Caio listened, rapt. The ease with which their bodies leaned toward each other—there was a certain familiarity between them.

Nush's belly crashed down like an elevator car whose strings had been cut. She couldn't help rolling the hem of her threadbare T-shirt up and down, couldn't help contrasting her "weird" outfit, her thick glasses, her uncontrollable hair, and—the worst—her tendency to hide in corners during meetings and parties and gatherings… against the polished and entirely social Laura.

"Are they…together?" she asked, hating the crack in her voice.

"Not yet, as far as I know," Yana said with the authority of a woman who always had her finger on the pulse of all the gossip. "But even you must agree that they could be the force that would appeal to the different factions at One-Tech. So if you want him, now's the time to— "

"I can't just…come on to him, Yana," Nush said, even her words faltering. The few times she'd tried to have sex—to get Caio out of her mind—had been utter disasters. She was beginning to wonder if she had some kind of mental block. If she tried it with Caio, she'd probably melt into a puddle of insecurities before she even touched him and further humiliate herself.

"Why not?" Her sister sounded genuinely confused.

"What if it destroys our relationship as it is?" she said, giving voice to her biggest fear. "I can't lose him."

Sympathy flared in Yana's eyes. "Then move on, Nush. Start living your own life instead of being a spectator in the margins of his."

"Why do you think I've been dating every Tom, Dick and Harry this past year? Why do you think I lasted weeks with Peter Jr. even though he makes me want to pluck my own eyeballs out?" That she'd hoped it would incense

Caio, who hated Peter Sr. and Jr. with the same loathing as they did him, Nush kept to herself. It felt more than a little twisted to let him direct who she dated but she'd done it anyway.

"Then be prepared to see them ride off into the sunset together, Nush. Who knows? You might get to be the flower girl at their wedding."

"I'm not a kid, Yana," Nush retorted, but she knew that Yana was right.

If nothing changed, she'd have to see him marry Laura or someone else equally perfect, drunk dance at his wedding because that was the only time she danced, buy his wife and him pretty crockery for a wedding gift, probably babysit his perfect kids and be their weird aunt who taught them coding in the summer and…

Nush shuddered. "Tell me what to do. Please."

"Seduce him."

The thought of his rejection—or worse, the thought of him laughing at her attraction to him—made hot acid gurgle up her throat. Her shoulders slumped as she realized her stupid fantasies would have to remain just that. She might be a genius when it came to computers and numbers but with Caio… "I can't, Yana. I don't think I can even put it in words."

Yana sighed and pulled her closer. "Nushiekins, you're beautiful and smart and kind and funny… Any man would be fortunate to have you in his life."

"You're my sister. You have to say that." Tears prickled and Nush blinked to keep them at bay. Maybe this was not only the year of loss but also of letting go. Of moving on. "What do I do, Yana?"

"If you can't face trying to seduce him, then break this hold he has on you. Decouple yourself from him and OneTech. Start a new branch in New York, or better yet, Switzerland. Go on a tour of the world. Have a scandalous fling or five. Step out of your lab and live your life, Nush."

By the time Caio reached her, Nush was trembling with the need for action. Marveling at how death and grief could fill one with a raw, painful urgency to live life. To move on.

Yana was right. She couldn't spend another minute much less a decade mooning over him. Couldn't stand still and be a spectator as he lived his life. Even now, she couldn't turn away as he finished his conversation with Laura and made his way to her.

As his tall form drew near, Nush noted the dark shadows under his eyes. He'd forgone a shave this morning. There was a tension to his shoulders that she recognized. Her heart ached as she remembered he'd been a part of her grandparents' life longer than she'd been.

She wanted to hold him through this aching emptiness Thaata had left in both their lives. She wanted to lean into him and help him through the grief she saw in his eyes.

But he wouldn't lean on her. Because he was the one who was supposed to be the protector. The one who looked after every legal headache that she and her sisters would have to handle. The one who'd arranged every single detail with the funeral. The one who'd made sure their alcoholic father had showed up to the funeral in respectable clothes and mostly sober.

Because Caio Oliveira didn't need anyone in any way. Least of all her. Even as he'd entrenched himself into the very fabric of her life. And it was time to rip him out of it.

He handed her a glass of water wordlessly and leaned against the wall beside her, their shoulders just touching. Resentment built in her chest even as she took the glass from him. How did he know there was a boulder-sized lump in her throat?

She didn't have to look at him to know he'd have pulled one foot up against the wall, that the other hand would be tucked into his pocket. That his gaze would sweep over the room, assessing the situation, wondering if there was a fire he'd have to put out.

His intense physicality, his indefatigable energy had always awed her. But now it felt exhausting to be so in tune with his every word, gesture and nuance, his very breath. More than disenchanting to admit that he'd never know her or want her on that level.

Holding that feeling close, Nush drank the water. As hard as it was to bear, it was the thing that would help her move on.

His shoulder nudged hers, his profile sharp and stark. "You're upset, Princesa."

Are you and Laura Huntington dating?

Have you had sex with her?

What do I do to make you see me like that?

Do you feel this too or is it just me?

Nush looked at the empty glass in her hand, following the trails of condensation, willing her body to ignore the warmth emanating from his. To not draw the scent of him into her lungs. To not chase this shaky desire she felt at his nearness like an addict. "Is there a reason you're stating the obvious?"

If he noted her bitchy tone, he ignored it. "What did Yana say to upset you?"

"Just bringing me up to speed on some politics at OneTech."

He tapped at her knuckles. "Don't worry about it, Nush. I'll handle it."

"Is Ms. Huntington joining the executive team?" The question escaped her before she'd decided to ask it.

He sent her a long, leisurely sideways look and Nush tried to not fidget. His surprise wasn't unwarranted. Usually, she stayed miles away from the politics of OneTech, happy to be in her lab. Thaata had tried numerous times to get her involved in the running of the company but she'd hidden. Usually behind Caio's broad shoulders. Had used him as a shield again and again.

"Probably. Laura, unlike her useless brother, would be a great addition to the team. For a Huntington, I like her immensely," he said with a grin.

He liked Laura. Immensely.

She couldn't remember a time when he'd actually said he liked a woman or a man. Outside of her sisters and her and their grandparents, he had no close friends. Not in any context. The long hours he worked made him just as much a loner as she was. And his family, she'd learned long ago, was a forbidden topic for all of them.

Her chest ached as if someone was pushing a tremendous weight down on her. Even with her eyes closed, she sensed him turn fully toward her. Felt his gaze sweep over her features. His fingers were firm as he lifted her fisted hand from her side. "What did your grandfather's note say?"

She jerked her hand away, giving him her shoulder. "It's private."

"Even to share with me?"

"Despite what you think, I have a life that doesn't revolve around you, Caio. Beyond being your good little worker droid, making you millions, I mean."

She sensed his shock in his sudden stillness. "Worker droid?" Cool, smooth tone still. "Jesus, you're more than upset if you think that's what I think of you. What's going on with you, Nush?"

"Leave me alone. Don't manage me. Don't—"

"Leaving you alone during this time is the last thing your grandfather would expect of me. Whatever's…bothering you, we can find a solution."

Was that all he saw her as? As a duty he owed to the man who'd loved him? As an obligation? "Did you make the same offer to Yana and Mira?"

"Look at me, Anushka."

She hated it when he said her name in that tone. As if she needed to be reprimanded. "Answer my question, Caio."

"No, I didn't."

"Why not?" she asked, genuinely curious.

What was the difference in how he saw her and her sisters? Where did that stem from?

More silence greeted her question.

"Because they're strong enough that they don't need your condescending advice and protection? Because they don't need you to look after them?"

"Cristo, Nush…"

Nush rubbed her hand over her face. God, she was just making a fool of herself. "I'm not myself…"

She felt his fingers on her shoulder, pressing gently. "You're not alone, Anushka. Not today, not in the future."

He didn't say more but she sensed his confusion. She never threw tantrums, or insisted on having things her way all the time like Yana did. Neither did she retreat behind a calm, indestructible facade like Mira so that no one could reach her behind it.

Maybe it was the fact that living with her volatile mother had taught her not makes waves, to be content with whatever life dealt, to curl herself into the smallest corner and be still. Maybe it was the fact that she'd learned to be self-sufficient, to find her happiness in books and computers from a young age. Most importantly, she never fought with anyone. Least of all Caio.

And yet now, it felt as if she'd been sleeping

like one of those princesses in the fairy tales. Hiding behind computer fandoms. Letting life pass her by.

"Princesa…look at me."

She looked up, every cell in her immediately responding to his tone. The impact of those thickly lashed deep-set eyes hit her hard. A sharp nose, rugged mouth…there was a sensuousness to him that drew her like no other man could.

Could he see he was the reason she was miserable? Could he hear the thundering of her heart when he stood so close? Could he feel the prickle of heat across her skin when he focused all that energy on her?

Standing this close to him, she could see the imperfections in his face too. She catalogued them, as if they'd help puncture her awareness of him.

The three-inch-long scar that cut across his upper lip that he'd told her he'd acquired in a fight with his older brother as unruly teenagers. The crooked tilt of his lips to one side when he smiled. The small nick under his jaw, which told her he must have cut himself recently.

"I think you should stop calling me that," she said, swallowing away the longing that rose through her.

His chin drew down, his expression taking

on that hard quality that he used in the board-rooms. "That's the most ridiculous thing you've ever said to me."

A steeliness had crept into his voice that made a knot tighten in her chest. He was a master of his emotions but she heard the crack in his temper. Well, that's what she'd wanted, wasn't it? For him to treat her like he did everyone else.

"You don't think I should have a choice in what you call me?"

His eyes swept over her, as if she was someone new. As if, if he looked hard enough, he should be able to see through her sudden resentment. "Why is what I call you a problem when it was never before?" His tone gentled immediately. "Is it because Rao called you that?"

"No. Because it's condescending and infantilizing and—"

"I have never condescended to you." There was anger in his tone now, and that it excited her was a sorry truth of her life. "And the second word…" he thrust a hand through his hair, "I don't think I even know what it means."

"You're right. It doesn't matter what you call me anyway because… I'm quitting."

He stilled and Nush could no more stop taking him in than she could stop breathing. It was like when she watched one of his old soccer games and then pressed play when he was midleap. The economy, the pure animal grace of his movements, the sudden explosion from a deceiving stillness…it had always captivated her. And it happened now, live.

All of that simmering physical energy focused on her like a laser beam. Digging. Probing. Searching. "Quitting what, Princesa?" The silky smoothness of his voice only served to betray his cold fury.

Nush swallowed but forced the words out. "The job. The company. The city even." *You.* "I can't do this anymore."

Yana was right. She had to quit him like an addiction—cold turkey. Now. Before it was too late. Nothing else had worked.

He was fully turned toward her now, shielding her from the room and curious eyes. Even now, even when she was fighting with him for no good reason as far as he knew, he sought to make sure she wasn't exposed. One hand on his hip, he rubbed at his forehead with another, a vertical ridge between his brows. "You're not making sense."

Nush's gaze drifted to his mouth set in an uncompromising flat line, to his chin with the perfect little dimple, to the corded column of his neck. To the tattoo peeking out from under the undone collar of his shirt. The tattoo she wanted to see and touch and…lick.

"I don't have to make sense to you, Caio, or do anything in my life with your permission… I don't owe you an explanation."

His fingers wrapped around her wrist as Nush attempted to move past him and she stumbled into his body. She gasped at the contact but when she looked into his eyes, pure frost looked down at her. His grip on her bare arm was firm but not tight. "That's where you're wrong, *querida*. You can rant and rave at me, you can use me as a punching bag to vent your grief if you wish, you can hide from your sisters and the entire world but at the end of day, at the end of the year…at the end of all this, you and I are in it together, Nush. You and I will make or break OneTech. That's what Rao meant for this to be even when he's gone—a partnership for the ages."

"A partnership for the ages—that sounds like a curse to me. A punishment."

His chin reared down, his mouth flattening. Nush regretted the words instantly.

Eyes searching his, she wondered at the taut mask he wore, at the unflinching sacrifices he made for his ambition. She'd never seen him with a steady girlfriend. Never heard him talk about marriage or a future. And yet he was ready to settle down with Laura. Another merger in his goal of…what?

What did Caio truly want?

"You don't need me around anymore. You've never really needed me, Caio. As for my brain, OneTech owns the patent on all my work anyway. I signed a noncompete clause years ago."

"Is that what you think, Nush? That I only value your brain and what it can make for me next?"

"I don't know what to think," Nush said, cutting her gaze away from him. "Thaata's gone and it's a good time as any for me to evaluate my life. See where I want to be in five years. I have to move on before you…"

His fingers tightened on her arm as he zoomed in on that like a predator pouncing. "Before I what?"

"Before you…" Her throat was dry and her heart was beating away and it felt like every raw, uncertain, inch of her was exposed to his bright golden eyes. "Before things change even more. Before I…" She pressed her forehead to his bicep, trembling at his nearness.

"Before you what, Nush?" he repeated softly, a muscle jumping in his jaw, his gaze pinning her to the spot.

She looked up and he was looking down at her and Nush thought her heart might jump out of her chest and shout out her last secret if he didn't let her go. And so she said the one thing that she knew would fracture that impenetrable armor of his. "Before I hate you, Caio. I want to leave before everything that's good and right between us rots and dies."

He released her so fast that she stumbled back. But in the next breath, his arm was around her waist, steadying her, letting her find her balance. Watching over her even as she made a fool of herself.

Weak and spineless as she was, Nush sought his gaze but he wasn't looking at her. His dismissal of her was as complete as she'd wanted it to be. And something between them broke and she wondered if that was the beginning of the end of the bond they'd always shared.

Tucking her arms tight around her midriff, she ran from the room. Heads turned, conversations stopped, whispers abounded but it didn't matter what anyone thought of her. Not when she knew in her heart of hearts that she was a coward.

Shaking her head at Mira, who'd only make her talk about it, Nush left the house.

Quitting…was the only course of action left to her.

Quitting working with him.

Quitting this first-row seat to his life.

Quitting Caio completely might be the only way she could break out of it.

CHAPTER TWO

CAIO OLIVEIRA WAS a man who was rarely ever shocked by life. Because he arranged for it to be exactly how he liked it. From the people he surrounded himself with—there were maybe four people in the world he allowed to speak their minds with him, one whose loss was eating through him—to how many more moves he needed to make to achieve his goal, to what kind of distractions he allowed in his life in the name of fun and play: everything was thought out, everything was calculated.

For more than a decade, he'd worked hundreds of hours a week to turn OneTech into the tech giant it was today. He'd taken risk upon risk, alienated most of the board members, fought and won countless battles with Rao to achieve the level of success he had. He'd never lost sight of his why though.

He could have stopped at any moment in the last few years. He'd never have to work in his life again if he stopped tomorrow and could still live a life of unprecedented luxury. But luxury and yachts and penthouses or acquisition of any other kind of material wealth had never driven him.

Only the need to prove himself after he'd been robbed of everything that had mattered to him, the need to exact revenge on the man who'd cast him out of his own home and his father's company, who'd destroyed his relationship with his mother.

And now, after years, he had what he'd wanted all these years within grasp. Almost. Another week and he'd have been able to acquire the software giant his stepfather operated out of Brazil.

Only Rao had passed away unexpectedly— before he could sell his stock to Caio—and while Caio had enough independent wealth to not need OneTech, he did need the clout he'd have as CEO of OneTech to acquire such a big company. To force his stepfather to sell it without knowing that Caio was pulling the strings meant using one of the subsidiaries that he and Rao had set up in Nush's name.

Right now, he needed to focus all his energies on retaining the CEO position on the board of OneTech. He needed to see Peter Huntingon Sr.'s cunning strategies and counteract them. And for that, if he needed to tie himself to the man's daughter—whom he'd been dangling in front of Caio—then so be it. He would let himself be chained to a woman even if he'd never had any intentions of marrying. At least he could tolerate Laura.

Except…for the bomb Anushka had dropped in his lap earlier. For now, he could go ahead with his plans without her standing by his side, absolutely. But…he wanted Nush on his side. By his side for this next leg of OneTech's journey.

And the fact that he did jarred him on levels he didn't want to examine right then.

The only thing that existed outside of this driving need to send his stepfather and his stepbrother to their knees was his relationship with Nush. The only person he'd allowed close—which was delusional in itself because it had happened without his knowledge or permission—the only person he could be someone else with other than a man driven by the need for revenge was Anushka.

Years ago, he'd stopped trying to control how their relationship evolved. Had admitted that somehow Nush had lodged herself under his skin, never to be pulled out.

From the moment he'd picked her up on that flight years ago to this evening when she'd suddenly turned on him…she'd been the one thing Caio had never been able to box into a grid in his life. Not even Rao had stitched himself up into the fabric of his life as Nush had.

A creature of habit, he was used to having her as a part of his life. Part of his inner circle—a circle of two, as Rao once had joked, when he'd found Nush and Caio laughing at something in the early hours of dawn at their respective workstations in her lab.

How dare she now change the rules on him?

He wanted to write off her sudden anger at him as her grief and loss taking over, but he hadn't been able to let it go. Hours had passed and it stung and poked like a rusted nail scratching under his skin. It infuriated him that she had such a hold on him and yet he hadn't been able to stop himself from seeking her out. From wanting to provide some kind of reassurance—like a codependent friend or worse a spurned lover—and demand it return that things between them would go back to as they'd been.

For months now, he'd sat back and watched as she'd distanced herself from him little by little. Had watched with more than a mild irritation and at times confused and misdirected fury, as she'd forced herself into a social life he knew she didn't want, as she'd dated and partied and entertained men like Peter Huntington Jr. Even though he knew she despised the kind of crowd that trust fund brat represented. Had suppressed the urge to ask her what the hell she thought she was doing with her life. Had reassured himself that the burn he felt in his gut when he saw her with a man was nothing but his overtly possessive, protective nature rearing its head.

When he'd brought up her sudden party animal behavior with her grandfather, Rao had smiled an infuriatingly cryptic smile and said his little Princess was testing her wings, whatever the hell that meant.

Caio remembered being baffled as to why sensible, smart Nush would indulge in things that didn't appeal to her in the first place. And the worst part, he'd felt a sense of disappointment in her, a strange, stinging sense of betrayal at how she'd started pulling away from him.

But enough was enough. To think of her new interests and distractions in life as a phase was one thing. But learning that she was unhappy to the point that she felt she had to walk away, that she'd even begun to hate him…that was intolerable. On some level, it felt like a personal failure.

He stilled outside Rao's study, hand raised for a knock, a new realization twisting through him with a crystal-clear clarity.

Anushka was his Achilles' heel.

The one person that made him act out of character. The one person with whom his relationship defied any sort of definition. And that should have sent him away, should have been warning enough.

But he didn't heed it.

Past midnight, Nush found herself walking through her grandfather's study like some night wraith. She'd been unable to sleep, the thought of leaving sending her mind in a thousand directions.

One hand wrapped around a warm mug of milk, she inhaled the scent of Thaata's hand-rolled cigars and something else.

It took her two breaths to figure it out.

Caio's scent. Of course, he'd been working out of here for a few months now. Jesus, wherever she went in this house, he was present to tease and taunt her.

His anger earlier in the evening had shocked her. Maybe because she'd never seen that cold will targeted at her. Maybe because she'd never really gone toe-to-toe with him. For a second, she'd even wondered if he could sense her frustration. If he could feel…

No.

God, she was just going in circles again and again. Driving herself out of her mind imagining things that weren't real.

Putting the mug away, she pulled her feet up and settled into the leather chair. The soft, worn leather enveloped her like an embrace she desperately needed. Closing her eyes, it was easy to imagine it was Caio's arms around her. With a choked cry, she bent her cheek to the desk.

And that was how Caio found her—rubbing her face against the rough grain of the dark oak desk he'd built with his own hands three years ago. Imagining it was those calloused fingers that stroked her.

The study door closed with a thud that made her heart follow with its own beat.

Heat and awareness charged each other across her skin as she felt his gaze take in the picture she made. Of her spaghetti top and skimpy shorts she hadn't covered up in her urgent need to escape her bed.

Arms hugging the cool wood, she stayed like that—trying to calm the ache in her breasts, the fire simmering in her belly, wondering if he'd leave. But he had every right to linger here, to mourn her grandfather and she wasn't going to push her company on him.

Straightening away from the desk, Nush got to her feet and walked around the desk on the opposite side.

"Don't leave on my account," he said, his tone smooth. His control firmly back in place. "Are you having trouble sleeping again?"

Her eyes got acclimated to the darkness as

she searched for him. Moonlight outlined his broad shoulders and tapered waist. "Yes. But I'll go back now."

When his hands moved to the light switch, she said, "No, don't. I'm not…dressed properly."

His surprise was a taut thread in the room, reaching for her, pulling at her.

Nush closed her eyes, wishing she hadn't said anything at all. It revealed too much of the thrumming awareness that touched her when he was near. Telling him it was hard to be around him right now was the grown-up thing to do. Instead, she was doing everything but. Playing a stupid game.

"Nush…"

"Please, Caio. I don't want to fight."

"As you wish, Princesa."

"Why are you so easygoing with me?" she asked, breaking her own rule. "I was the one who behaved illogically earlier. The one who came at you out of nowhere."

She could see that vertical ridge between his brows again. "What?"

"You are different with everyone else. Even with Thaata, I think. You never give an inch, Caio. You're arrogant, demanding, ruthless even. Yana, I know, is definitely a little scared of you. But with me…a different side of you comes out.

You're gentle, understanding, far too accommodating. Even when I'm behaving like a brat."

He laughed and she let it envelop her like a lover's embrace. His embrace. "My father would have enjoyed to hear me being called accommodating."

The clear affection in his tone was a pleasant surprise. Nush hugged the piece of information to herself, hoarding pieces of the puzzle she'd long wanted to solve. "Exactly," she said, a glimmer of her smile coating her words. "So why?"

"You resent me for treating you differently." He stated it baldly, as if he'd only now arrived at that irrevocable conclusion. "Here I thought you were the most uncomplicated woman I've ever known, Nush."

"At least you think me a woman," she mumbled to herself and then prayed to the laws of physics that he hadn't heard her. Clearly, her filter was completely off today.

His head cocked to the side and all Nush wanted to do was to run her fingers over the corded column of his throat. "Do you remember the first time I came to pick you up?"

Nush nodded. That summer had been one of the best of her life. Not only had she spent every minute with Mira and Yana but she'd also started working with Caio. Her grandparents had spent hours with her. Even their dad had dropped in for a few visits. For the first time in her life, Nush had found total acceptance, even when she was at her weirdest.

"You were terrified of leaving your mom behind. You were desperate to see Yana and Mira and your grandparents. You said you couldn't wait to spend every day making memories to take back with you for when you needed them. You...tried to be strong and brave even when you didn't have control of anything around you. You...reminded me of myself. Of who I'd been before I lost all semblance of innocence and good. Of who I'd been a long, long time ago. Sometimes, I wonder if..."

Nush didn't say anything, so afraid that if she interrupted him, he might stop talking. He might stop sharing. He might stop giving her this little glimpse into his head.

"There's an untouched innocence to you that none of us have been able to hold on to. I know Rao and Mira, and even Yana, feel as if they could do anything to keep that part of you safe. It's the same thing that makes me feel protective of you. Maybe because no one looked out for me. I lost so much...that I can never get back. Even if I wanted it back."

A dark thread of anger vibrated in the last sentence. As if he hadn't quite let go of it, even as he acknowledged that it had changed him for the worse.

Nush wrapped her arms around her knees on the chair and studied him with her chin tucked into them. It was the most he had ever shared about his background. "I'm sorry that you were alone when you needed someone. I know how terrifying that feels."

"I know you do, Princesa." He sighed then, and it rattled in the quiet between them. "Just because I feel protective of you doesn't mean I think any less of you, Anushka."

A sudden, strange warmth came over her, leaving her trembling in its wake. Their eyes met in the darkness and Nush nodded, not trusting her voice. The silence that followed had an unusual thrumming quality to it for two people who were used to spending hours together in companionable silence. Like there were things being said without either of them saying it. And she wondered if it was her betraying herself. Wondered if the truth of her desire for him could be worse than this…strange game she was playing.

She watched as he moved around the room, touching Thaata's things just as she'd done before he'd arrived. Only now, when that shamefully needy part of her had been assuaged with his words, did she note how on edge his movements were. How unsettled the energy around him felt when he usually didn't let anything fracture his determination toward his end goal.

When he reached the other side of the desk and picked up the framed picture of her and Caio standing on either side of her grandfather—one that had been taken last year—she let out a shuddering breath. His fingers moved over her grandfather's face in the picture, his gaze far away.

"Tell me how you came to know Thaata," she said, wanting to give him something for once, wanting to take away the far-off look in his eyes.

A sudden smile simmered into existence, a pocket of light in the darkness around them. "It was Rao who came to my rescue when I didn't have anything or anyone. When I hated the world and wanted to burn it down. And I didn't make it easy for him either."

"He never told me that. Don't tell me you and Thaata used to fight?"

"All the time, especially when he brought me here in the beginning. I was like an out-of-control, festering wound. I didn't want to trust him. It was only after I'd spent several days with Yana and Mira that I believed that he meant well. That he did care about me."

"Why did he come to your...rescue?" She searched his face, desperate to see every nuance in those eyes. "I can't imagine you needing rescue in any way."

He rubbed a hand over his face. Exhaustion she'd never seen before was etched into the gesture. "I can't imagine how bad my life could've gotten if he hadn't."

Her heart ached to see him like that. "You mean you weren't born arrogant and confident and ruthlessly perfect?"

"Perfect, *querida*? Far from it." She heard his laughter and his shock in his response. "Rao and my dad worked together as entry-level engineers a long time ago when they'd both been trying to make it here. They even started their companies at the same time, Papa back in Brazil and Rao here. They kept in touch until Papa passed away when I was nine. Rao checked on me and Mama regularly. He never forgot about us." Caio sounded faraway and tense, as if the memories weren't good ones. "When I had nowhere to go, Rao invited me to come work for him. All based on a relationship with a man who was long gone."

Nush smiled. "I hope you know he wasn't being altruistic. Thaata must have known what a fantastic investment you'd turn out to be. He once told me that he hadn't imagined a tenth of the success you've made of OneTech."

Fingers tracing the edge of the desk, Caio

walked around until he was leaning against it, within her reach. "Oh, I've no doubt of that. Rao was a long-term strategist. His trust in me… I can't tell you what it meant to me. But Rao believed in second chances and that's what landed us in this mess with Peter Sr. too."

"Is that why no amount of success is enough, Caio? Because you have to pay it back in spades? Why you'll go to any lengths to keep your control of OneTech intact?"

"Now you even sound like your grandfather," he said, easily sidestepping her question. Shock swept through her as she realized that each word of his was measured, everything he'd shared had been calculated to get something back. "I find it amazing how much of him there is in you. He was a pioneer and didn't let anything bother him when he was in that lab and was unrelentingly stubborn when he got a notion into his head."

And just like that, he reminded Nush of what she had to do. For her own sake. "Then you also know that I don't make decisions easily, Caio. I have to leave. Though…" she stared at her fingers bathed in moonlight, careful with her own words now, "I'm sorry for how I spoke to you earlier. It was unfair. You made a convenient target for something that wasn't your fault."

"You're sorry for the how, but not for what you said," he observed drily, almost in a matter-of-fact voice. As if he was sifting and separating her intent from her words. "You meant it when you said you'd begin to hate me if you stayed. Or do you hate me already, Princesa?"

And suddenly, Nush realized that he'd come in search of her—not just found her—that their conversation—one she'd foolishly instigated—was far from over. That he wouldn't rest until he knew all about her secret fascination with him.

This was the Caio she knew—a man who never left a stone unturned if it caught his interest. Except it was all directed at her now.

"I don't hate you." She turned her gaze to the desk, afraid of what he'd see in her expression. "I didn't know what I was saying."

"Wrong, Nush. For the first time in months, I think you were being truthful with me."

Of course, he'd noticed that she'd been avoiding him little by little for months now. The only time she hadn't been successful in completely avoiding him was when they worked together on the software solution for a ten-billion-dollar contract her design had won.

Nush tilted her chin up. "I'm twenty-three, Caio. I've been working in one form or the other for a decade now. Between Mama and OneTech and evening classes, I've barely had a life of my own. Wanting to change it up is not so…unreasonable."

"But you fixed that with a very busy social life this past year, no?"

Heat claimed Nush's cheeks at his wry comment that he'd taken note. She had gone on date after date, plastered herself at parties Yana had dragged her to, danced at clubs even though she hated that kind of mindless chitchat and search for familiarity with strangers, given out her number to anyone who'd asked, determined to get over this stupid crush. "It wasn't enough. It didn't fix what I wanted to fix."

"I need more, Nush."

Her head jerked up, something in his tone making every sense come alert and alive. "What do you mean?"

"If you're going to hate me and clearly, you're halfway there, I think it's more than fair that I know the reason. I'd like to know why you think our relationship is...*rotting.*"

Cold fury thrummed along each word out of his mouth and yet, Nush had a feeling it was directed at himself rather than her. For the hundredth time that day, she wondered if she knew Caio at all.

"What have I done to upset you so, Princesa?" The words seemed to be wrenched out of him against his will.

She swallowed helplessly, wondering what she'd set into motion. "You didn't do anything wrong, Caio. Please…believe me, it's all me. Me and my stupid…"

Suddenly, the lamp on the desk was turned on and golden light warmed her face and he was standing too close and…there was no way to avoid looking at him. Or to stop him from seeing her. Everything she felt and wanted and craved would be written in her face.

But she remained rooted to the spot, studying him in turn.

Dressed in dark gray sweats and an anime print T-shirt she'd printed for him, he looked like a dark angel demanding answers she didn't want to give. Of cheap quality, the tee had long faded, leaving the short sleeves and chest pulling tight against his defined body.

Her breaths turned shallow when he turned the leather chair.

"The truth, Anushka."

Her name, this time, was a warning and she realized with a surge of disbelief that she'd wounded him that evening. Her words of hate and resentment had found a weak spot in the mighty and ruthless Caio Oliveira's armor and drawn blood. She didn't know why, didn't know how she knew, didn't care if he was aware of it.

And even as an irrational, selfish part of her gloried in the fact that she'd at last reached him in that twisted way, a big part of her disliked herself for her willful words. She wasn't the kind of woman who took out her frustration on others. She didn't want to be full of bitterness like her mother. She didn't want to hurt the man who'd always stood by her side for more than a decade—through hardships and successes—a man who'd been kind to her, again and again, because he thought she held some indefinable quality he himself had lost.

She looked up to find him staring at her, the gold of his eyes darkening, his nostrils flaring. "I've already lost Thaata and the thought of losing you too makes me—" Tears filled her eyes and the sob she'd been fighting since Thaata's stroke, since her grandmother's death, and Mama's deteriorating health, broke through her paltry defenses.

She closed her eyes and tried to fight it, but her throat burned and Caio was there pulling her into in his arms and there was no stopping the dam from bursting. They came in hot rivulets, of grief and loss, of bone-deep fear that everyone she loved would leave her. That she'd always be lonely and unwanted and that years would pass by and she'd never even act on…

"Shh… Princesa," Caio kept whispering, his arms a loose but comfortable weight around her shoulders. "You're not losing me, Nush."

His body was a hard shield around her that

could keep all her troubles at bay. It was the kind of thinking that had got her into this mess, but right now, she couldn't care.

For a long while, Nush stayed in his embrace, letting the solid weight of him soothe her. She knew she'd left splotchy wetness on his tee, but she didn't want to move. Not yet. Not when she might not have a right to hold him like this ever again. Not when he was busy spinning strategies, making new alliances that would push her out of his life.

Her fingers gripping his biceps, her cheek pressed to his chest, she inhaled deep, willing some of that impenetrable strength into her.

A pure, untarnished moment of comfort and security and peace that she'd rarely known in her life. And she wondered if that was the reason for her attraction to him—that Caio presented an indefatigable promise of constancy, an indomitable presence in her life that she'd never had with anyone else.

Eventually, her tears dried up, and something else simmered in her veins. Like the flickering light of a candle, desire she'd tried to hide so hard for months roared to life. It was impossible to fight it when she'd programmed her brain to find the very scent of him arousing, intoxicating. And now all she could smell and touch and feel were the hard contours of him reshaping her softness to fit him.

Nush tightened her arms around him and moved her face up into his neck, into the hollow at his throat. Moved her lips against the corded column of his neck, let the taste of his skin and sweat and *him* seep into her. For no longer than a breath's span, she lingered over that hard line between them, an airy lightness fizzing through her.

She heard the indrawn hiss of Caio's breath, the hard clench and release of his body around her. His hands gripped her hips, tight and arresting.

"Nush?" His eyes searched hers in the darkness, his features woven tight into a forbidding mask that locked up every emotion.

Even now, fear and cowardice urged her to laugh it off. To act like it was unintentional, that she was mindless in her grief. Sweat dampened the nape of her neck and her forehead.

No, she batted away at her fears.

There was nothing wrong with her desire for him. Nothing wrong that she wanted him. And God, she was tired of fulfilling that desire with men she wasn't even interested in. Of hiding what she felt. Of telling herself that it wouldn't work. Of running away from life.

CHAPTER THREE

STILL, NUSH'S SENSE of right and wrong would let her go only so far when all he offered was comfort. Words were needed and even though she hated forming them, releasing them, she knew it was time.

"I…want this, Caio, with you." Slowly, bracing herself to be pushed away, feeling as if her very existence was contingent upon touching him, she pressed her forehead to his chin.

He didn't blink or sigh or push her away and she let it all out. "I've spent months telling myself that it can't happen, that you don't see me like that, that it's madness to want you." A laugh escaped her mouth and still he didn't move or say anything and some spark of hope lit up inside her and she kept running toward the edge, rearing to jump off the cliff. "This is why I want to leave, why I find it unbearable to be near you." Another wretched sound escaped her and she bunched her hands in his shirt. "And now to know that you might be making… Do you see why I have to leave? Why I can't be here while you make new…alliances? It would be easier on me to hate you, Caio, than to—"

"Cristo," Caio said in a low, guttural growl and his head jerked down and she jerked her head up and his chin bumped her cheekbone and pain jarred through her and his fingers were over her cheek and she was breathing hard, trying to untangle herself and his hands were over her shoulders and then her mouth went flush against his.

She might have stopped breathing altogether, her heart stopping its frenzied beating. Everything in her stilled to better drink in the sensation of his mouth against hers.

And for the first time in months, she felt as if she'd reclaimed a part of her she hadn't even realized she'd lost. She wanted to own this desire. Own her choices, right or wrong, successful or full of defeat. "I don't want this to be some accident. Don't want you to say this was some kind of overflow from all the grief and loss of the last few months. It's not. This is what I've wanted for…months now, Caio. I want to kiss you. Now. I want to see if you…feel this thing too. I want to test this pull I feel. Or I'll regret not taking the risk forever."

Waiting for him to push her away or walk

away was the hardest thing Nush had ever done in her life. But he didn't. Only stared at her, those golden flecks in his eyes darkening, his nostrils flaring, his entire frame tense and tight.

Letting him see the want in her eyes was the biggest, headiest rush. More than a rough, hungry kiss with another man. More than half-naked groping in the dark with a stranger.

One breath turned into the next and the next, and Nush sank her fingers into his thick hair, pulled his head down and pressed her mouth to his.

Still, he watched her, an inherent challenge in that taut jaw line, the gold of his eyes darkening. And that was its own aphrodisiac, winding her up, taunting her to rise to the occasion. Heat burned through her, leaving every doubt and insecurity in piles of ashes. She glided her mouth from one end of his to the other, rubbed up and down, sucked his lower lip between hers and then his upper. Their noses bumped, their breaths a loud whistle in the room.

Textures and sensations assaulted her, all at once. The contrast of his rough stubble and the softness of his lips made a soft moan escape her. Needing more, she explored every inch of his mouth, every slope and rise and dip and curl, the rigid contour of his upper lip and the lush give of his lower lip.

Desire trickled through her limbs like warm honey, dripping and pooling in her lower belly. Hotter and needier and hungrier and…he was kissing her back. He had been kissing her back from the first contact.

Only now, in true Caio fashion, he was taking control of the kiss.

Her pulse drummed in her ears as Nush took a hasty catalog of the new sensations vying for attention.

His fingers in her hair, gripping firmly, holding her for his onslaught, his other hand cupped her hip nudging her closer, her small breasts crushed against his hard chest and his mouth… God, his mouth. It was everything she'd ever dreamed of, his kiss hotter and filthier than her wildest fantasy.

She was panting, every muscle trembling, her skin burning up as he chased and hunted and devoured her lips, not letting her settle into or savor any one sensation. He nipped at her lower lip and he licked the hurt when she mewled and he growled against her mouth until the sheer vibrating pulse of it made her open her mouth with an answering groan. And then his tongue was swooping into her mouth. Cajoling, teasing, taunting, licking, his hands moved all over her back and the more he took and demanded and wanted, the more Nush wanted to give.

Desire made her dizzy, and she clung to him, digging her fingers into his shoulders, scratching her nails into his scalp. Throwing all her weight onto him, she nudged her hips forward and the heated press of his erection against her lower belly created the most delicious burn between her thighs.

"Caio," she whispered, sobbing and panting his name, begging for release.

It was the wrong thing to say, the wrong thing to invoke. The spell broke, as suddenly and violently as the kiss had taken off.

Caio's sudden stillness was like a cold splash of water over her heated skin. *"Merda!"*

The word reverberated between them before he set her back from him in such a sudden movement that Nush crashed into the hard, sharp edge of the desk behind her.

With another rough sounding curse, Caio reached out to steady her. But his fingers landed her hip and Nush jumped away with a gasp of pain.

"Wait, Princesa. Don't move." Going to his knees in a sinuous movement, he lifted the edge of her spaghetti top and tugged the hem of her shorts down gingerly. Even in the dark, Nush could see the blue-green bruise already taking shape.

"Cristo!" Caio stared at the flare of her hip

where the bruise was. One long finger traced the edges of it before he muttered, "I didn't mean to…hurt you." Deep and hoarse and guttural, his voice pinged over her.

Nush bit her lip, trying to ignore the sensation of his fingers on her bare skin. Or how her sex clenched greedily at the sight of him on his knees in front of her, his mouth inches from flesh she'd caressed while thinking of him. "It's okay," she murmured, wanting to sink her fingers into his hair again but not daring. To touch him—even after their explosive kiss—was an intimacy she hadn't been granted yet. Her skin tingled as he stayed like that, head dipped, the remnant warmth of their kiss burning like embers within her limbs. "It just hurt a little when you grabbed me." She couldn't help pushing back a lock of hair that had fallen onto his forehead. "I'm fine."

His fingers arrested her wrist. "This is what will happen if we do this, *querida*."

"What?"

"I'll hurt you."

"You're being ridiculous," Nush said, striving for a levity she didn't feel. "It was an accident."

He sprang to his feet and away from her with that grace that, for once, couldn't hide the fact that he didn't want her to touch him anymore.

Nush stayed still, hope deflating inside her

chest as fast as it had grown. Dread chased away every spark of pleasure. She'd thought to let him know of her desire, to let him see it, to find out that he didn't return her interest, or that he didn't feel the same attraction would be the hardest part of this.

But it wasn't. It was this waiting.

That Caio had kissed her back, that even now his broad frame shook with tension was easy to see. That she'd only felt a part of something that had already existed between them was clear.

But waiting for his reaction to what they'd done, waiting to see what he'd say to her in the wake of the best kiss of her life…this was the hardest part. She felt as if her vulnerability was written all over her face, a giant neon sign waiting for his decision.

For long seconds, he looked at that framed photo of the three of them again.

"Caio?"

A rough thrust of his fingers through his hair. When he spoke, he sounded cool, distant. As if the kiss hadn't affected him at all. "I should've stopped you. I will regret it for the rest of my life that I didn't."

Nush flinched as if he'd dealt her a body blow.

Caio wished he could take back the words instantly.

Cristo, he was full of a contrariness that he couldn't fathom. He didn't want to hurt her. Ever. And yet, that meant hurting her now. Killing the hope he saw in her eyes now before it was too late.

"That can't happen again, Nush," he said softly.

"And yet, it just did." Her chin tilted up in a stubborn streak he knew so well. "You kissed me back. And you enjoyed the hell out of it. I've kissed enough men to know the difference."

"I don't need a reminder of your colorful love life of the past year," he said, the taste of her on his lips a teasing promise he wanted to explore further.

Something glinted in her eyes, a flash of such pure satisfaction, that it was only then Caio realized how…judgmental and even a little jealous he sounded.

The situation was unraveling, getting away from him faster than he could fix it. And it made him lash out in a way that he'd never been with her. He did it even though he hated himself for the cruelty in his words. "I was taken by surprise. You were crying and I didn't want to upset you further by pulling away."

"You're a bastard," she said, her chin rearing down. "How dare you twist something so real up like that?"

"You have no idea how close to truth you are in your assessment, Princesa. I'm a bastard when things don't go my way. Let's do each other a favor and forget it ever happened."

Shoulders straightened, stretching the tee tight across her chest until he could see the sharp points of her nipples. Eyes swollen from having cried, mouth pink from his kisses, hair a haphazard halo around her face, she looked like one of those mythical warrior women she became in her role-playing games. The stubborn streak that made her survive without breaking would never take his suggestion sitting down. He couldn't stop admiring the quality even as he needed to push her away.

"Admit that you lost yourself to the kiss as much as I did, that you want this as much as I do. If I hadn't moaned out your name and broken the spell, you'd have been f—"

"There is no this, Nush," he bit out, his voice low and urgent. "You and I can't…happen."

She blinked. Studied him thoughtfully. He could almost see her consider this from all points, gather her arsenal, make logical leaps. Damn it, that she approached this with the weight and logic and thought she gave everything made him want to kiss and rumple her all over. "I'm not asking you to marry me, Caio."

"What are you asking me then?" The question left his mouth against his wishes. An arrow shooting out of the dark, slumbering place that was remembering how she'd felt in his arms. How she'd responded to every caress. How she'd melted against him. How, even now, he wanted to hear from her own lips what she wanted of him, what she'd wanted of him. "What is it that you think I'm denying you?"

She licked her lips, her gaze zeroing on his own. Lust was a sizzling burn in his limbs as his libido made leaps he'd never before made. "I…"

Hesitation danced in her eyes and he gobbled it up like the big bad wolf he was. Who did she think he was? A hero straight out of those fairy tales who'd give her a happily-ever-after? One of those honorable knights she was so fond of reading about? Maybe that was the problem. "A red-hot affair? A fling that would cheapen everything we mean to each other? A quick fuck against the wall in this room that belonged to the man we both lost?"

"Don't bring Thaata into this."

"You're his precious granddaughter. He's in the middle of everything you and I do." He let out a long sigh, willing himself to appeal to her rationality. "I can't dishonor Rao's memory like that. I can't…dishonor you like that."

She stared at him, aghast. "My honor's not tied to my having sex. With you or anyone."

"I wholeheartedly agree, *querida*. But mine is tied to not taking advantage of the generosity and trust Rao gave me. In not taking advantage of your…affection for me."

"You really think I can't separate lust and affection? Grief and loss from want? Is that what you're afraid of? That if we have sex, I'll somehow confuse my poor unsuspecting mind and cling to you and make all sorts of demands on you? And for Thaata's sake and your poor honor's sake, you'll have to agree and be tied down to me for the rest of our lives?"

That the idea of being tied down to Nush for the rest of their lives didn't alarm him much alarmed him. He was really due for some mindless entertainment if his mind was making outrageous leaps like that out of thin air.

"What if we do have sex? Then what, Anushka? Do we greet each other as friends when it's over? Do we continue working and collaborating as if we don't know each other intimately? What happens when I have my fun with you, discard you and move on to the next woman that catches my fancy? Do you expect me to hold you together? Do you know if you can bear it when I lose interest in you and dump you?" He forced himself to be as crude as possible. "Because you know very well, that's what I do. Are you telling me you'd be okay with fracturing everything good between us…all for what? For a few minutes of mindless sex?"

"Yes, I want it as long as both of us want it. I want it because…" Some sort of self-preservation seemed to have caught her there. Swallowing, she looked down at her hands, and then back up at him. "Don't use Thaata or our relationship or your bloody integrity as excuses, Caio, because that's all they all are. If you don't want to pursue this, just say that. I'm mature enough to accept that."

So be it then. "Kissing you back was the biggest mistake of my life. I have plans for it that don't involve messing up what you and I might have in pursuit of questionable pleasure. I'm not some errant knight that will hold you together when an affair ruins things between us, Princesa. Your little experience with men doesn't mean you're ready for me. The fact that you hold one kiss so high in your estimation is proof enough of how naive and unworldly you are."

Even in the meager light of the table lamp, Caio could see how she paled. How that final barb had landed hard. Now that he was so in tune with her very breath, he could see the soft gasp that escaped her lush mouth.

Fat tears pooled in her eyes, magnified by the thick glasses. She blinked and one rolled down the very cheek he wanted to touch and clasp and hold. He'd always been the one who'd offered her a shoulder when she cried, who stood by her until she found that strength again. Never the one who made her cry and it left the foulest taste in his mouth.

"I have no use for you as a lover, Nush."

"No. Only for my brain in your campaign for world supremacy," she said with a scornful laugh.

It cut through him easily, her self-deprecation, her hot anger, her bitterness, like a knife through butter. And that he'd let her get so close to wound him shocked him in itself. "Princesa—"

"Stop." Finally, she blinked, pulled in a shuddering breath, straightened her shoulders and faced him. Always fighting, even in defeat, full of that steely strength that he'd always admired. "Get out, Caio."

He regarded the picture she made for several seconds, desperate to kiss away the hurt from her mouth. Cristo, he was screwed up in every way when it came to Nush.

He walked out, closing the door behind him. He'd spent a lot of time in the last fifteen years disliking who he'd become, but he'd never actively hated himself as much as he did then.

And while he knew he'd acted for the best, for both of them, Caio had a feeling he'd destroyed whatever they'd had and whatever they might have had. But the second was only possible if he'd been a better man.

CHAPTER FOUR

THE KISS STAYED with Caio for hours, days, taunting him, haunting him, mocking his so-called steely will, now lying in shredded ribbons at Nush's feet. Or was it at that luscious mouth and eager response that it was snagged on…

His week had been busy with media interviews, board meetings, figuring out which board members still respected Rao's vision for the company *and* supported Caio's position as CEO, versus which men were ready to jump ship.

He shouldn't have had a moment's quiet to dwell on the kiss. *Or her.* And yet it came to him, at the most unsuspecting of times, halting his thoughts, making him sprawl back and live it all over again.

Her bold declaration that she'd not let him call it something else, the perfect fit of her lithe body against his, the way she'd responded to his caresses, her moans, her fierce demands—he was never going to forget how she'd melted into him.

Every time he saw her, he'd see her as she'd been in that darkness.

Eyes big and wide behind those glasses, mouth trembling, nipples grazing his chest in pleasurable torment, the lush flare of her hips in his hands, the toned length of her thighs molding against his...

He pushed a hand through his hair. God, he was obsessing over a kiss.

Cursing his fractured discipline, Caio forced himself to think of the upcoming reading of Rao's will tomorrow. Once that was out of the way and Caio had the majority he needed, he needn't look back. Putting the purchase of his stepfather's company through to his CFO would be his first order.

And it wasn't just that he needed OneTech.

OneTech needed him too. Especially if he wanted to stop Peter Sr. from turning it into a cash cow with no principles or integrity.

Caio had lost not just a mentor and an investor and a professional colleague he respected, but a man who'd given Caio a purpose when he'd been sorely lacking one.

Being a part of Rao's family had given him a balance, a hope that he could build something after he achieved his goal. That he wasn't completely lost.

I've wanted this...for months, Caio.

Anushka's whispered declaration tugged at him. A vague shape of a wish teased at the edge of his consciousness and he batted it away.

Had she wanted him even as she'd dated other men?

And what do you feel about her? an insidious voice whispered much as he tried to bury it.

He let out a filthy curse that would have scandalized his mother. As rowdy as he and his brothers had been, Mama had been proud of the fact that she'd taught them manners. She'd also taught him what honor meant though only a frayed thread remained. Which said he couldn't use Nush like that.

And if that meant she hated him, so be it. If that meant they had to delete ten years of a fond, fulfilling relationship and start over as strangers, then so be it. With a ruthless will that had seen him through dark times, Caio pushed the thought of her out of his head.

It was early morning the day Rao's will was to be read while Caio was breakfasting on the veranda that looked out onto the beautiful blue of the ocean when he saw Nush.

Gritting his teeth, he tried to stop his gaze from sweeping all over her. It was a losing fight. Cristo, he'd never be ready for the sudden punch of desire that knocked him for sixes when he laid eyes on her now.

He let out a filthy curse under his breath, only realizing now how much damage the damned kiss had done. There was no going back from it. No unseeing Nush as the woman who'd so boldly declared she wanted him, who'd let him see the yearning in her eyes, who'd responded like dry tinder to fire to his every caress.

Who'd once again claimed him—whether he'd wanted to be or not—like no one else ever had.

She'd just returned from a morning run and was stretching on the lawn, chest heaving, long thigh muscles shaking. Unaware of what a delectable reward she provided him after three days of searching for her face wherever he went like some rejected loser.

He shouldn't want to look and even if he did, the decent thing would've been to look away. To not let one moment's bad decision compound into setting into motion things he couldn't take back as easily. Caio didn't even try.

She was wearing a burnt-orange sports bra and loose black shorts—an outfit he'd seen her in countless times. But this morning, he noted the swell of her small breasts pushing up and out of the bra as her chest heaved, the tight nip of her waist and the voluptuous flare of her hips, the sweet curve of her ass and those legs…she had the longest legs with toned muscles where her shorts rested. The silky sheen of miles of brown skin, begging to be touched and kissed and marred at his fingers...he swallowed.

Her thick, wavy hair pulled away from her face in a braid made that innocent sensuality she possessed shine brighter, hotter. Curly tendrils escaping it kissed the nape of her neck and she angrily pushed them into the braid in stabbing motions that made him smile.

All Caio wanted was to walk toward her and enfold her in his arms from behind. Wrap that thick braid in his hand and twist it up and away until he could see into those beautiful brown eyes. Kiss the sweaty curve of that elegant neck and taste the salt on her skin until she melted into him again. Run his hands down her body, stroke every dip and flare and inch of bare skin, learn where she was most sensitive.

He was semi-hard already, just from watching her. Just from knowing that she wouldn't stop him if he gave in to the madness and did any of those things.

And as arousing as that was, it was also the thought that cut through the haze.

There was nothing in the world that Nush did without giving it her all, without feeling it to the core of that steely sweetness. There was nothing he could give her but pain and hurt and...misery in the end. No promise he wouldn't break. No guarantee that he wouldn't ruin that sweet innocence of hers.

He was cynical to his core, and was even now making plans to ruin his stepfather. She'd be horrified when she learned he'd been planning such destruction for years, when she saw him for who he was truly then.

As if aware of his eyes on her, she turned mid-stretch. Across the few feet that separated them, their gazes met and held. Electricity arced between them, fueled by desire and something more, something he preferred to leave unsaid. Forever, if possible.

He cut his gaze away but it didn't go that far. Nothing, it seemed, when it came to Anushka, was in his control anymore.

Her face was pink and sweaty from the run. Without the glasses, her eyes looked enormous in her face. Suddenly he wondered why she didn't wear contacts or get it corrected by laser surgery. Suddenly there were too many things he didn't know about her.

Her throat moved on a hard swallow, calling his attention to the thin golden chain she wore with a pendant that said *Princesa* in gold. It was the only jewelry he'd ever seen her wear on a constant basis. A paltry gift he'd bought her for her sixteenth birthday that she'd always cherished. The weight of that was as terrifying as it was exciting.

Only your gift that she cherishes so much, a sneaky voice said in his head.

He wondered at how protective, even possessive he felt about her when he was determined to nip this thing between them.

"Good run?" he asked, determined to bring things back to some kind of even keel. Maybe it was a fool's wish but a part of him wanted that easy camaraderie they'd shared for almost a decade. He craved to be the Caio he'd been with her—fun, easygoing, free of the bitterness that had long tainted him.

Without answering, she lifted the navy-blue bottle of water and took a long chug.

Caio followed the trail of a water drop down her chin, down her long, elegant neck down to her cleavage where it disappeared. He should feel shame for watching her like that, and yet he didn't. There was no turning off the desire her kiss had unleashed.

When she finally joined him at the table, something in him calmed. Pulling a plate toward her, she applied a liberal amount of butter to her toast and then scooped three spoons of strawberry jam on top. Her sweet tooth and her utter enjoyment of food had always been something to watch. But now, there was a sensual element to it that made every muscle in him tight.

He closed his laptop with a loud thunk, giving up even the pretense of working.

Licking a clump of jam from her lower lip, she said, "If I'm disturbing you, I can leave."

If it had been anyone but her, Caio would've known that the gesture and the question were designed to go together. That she didn't realize how tempting and taunting she sounded only made him want her more. As if her innocent sensuality had been shaped to perfectly counteract his cynical disillusion of life. Even sex had at some point become boring, nothing but an exercise to relieve stress.

With Nush though, it would be hot and real and…raw.

He had the sudden, overwhelming urge to pull her into his lap and lick at that lower lip. To inhale the sweet taste of her mouth into him until he never forgot. To unravel her all over again.

"Caio?"

"Of course you're not disturbing me," he said, wondering if this was the hell his mother had warned him about ending up at when he'd get into nasty fights with his stepbrother Enzo The ones Enzo had always started, provoked Caio into, by spewing obscenities about Papa. "I'm never unavailable to you, Princesa."

She arched her brows and he realized he'd suggested something he hadn't meant to. Another bite of the toast followed before she said, "Did you need me to sign anything else? I asked your PA to check with you."

Irritation enveloped him instantly, a dark cloud. "You're still determined to leave?"

"Yes."

That's it. No qualification. No explanation.

Anger burned through Caio in fierce rivulets. But it was different from the bitterness he'd nursed for so many years. This was…pure, even selfish, a challenging burn he welcomed. "On that ridiculous yacht party with Peter Jr. and his deadbeat friends?"

"Do you want me to run my itinerary by you?" she said with exaggerated sweetness.

The minx was baiting him. Fine, if she wanted to play games, he would.

"You won't even stay for the reading of the will?"

She shrugged. "There's no real need for me to be there, right? Thaata's stock in OneTech would go to you. Mira, Yana and I will inherit various other assets. Just as he and you planned."

"You know, the more you hang out with that crowd, the more you're beginning to sound like a trust fund brat. Full of privilege and disregard for anything that doesn't touch you directly."

"That's unfair."

Some devil in him wanted to goad her, wanted to punish her for making him want something he couldn't have. "Is it? You know OneTech is in the middle of a hostile takeover that Peter Sr. has been planning from the moment he heard Rao's sick. Do you give a damn about Rao's vision? About the hundreds of employees whose fate hangs in the balance? About all the programs that Rao and I implemented that will eat dust if Peter wins the takeover and kicks me out?"

"I'm sure you have a plan to stop him from all of it. Important, life-altering plans," she bit out, throwing his words back at him. "I wasn't begging for reassurance when I said you never needed me. As to me being privileged…if that's how you truly see me, then screw you. I've never taken anything Thaata gave us for granted. I've even fought with him over who pays Mama's astronomical clinic bills and won. I've worked, just as hard as you have, over the last decade. In fact, that's all I have done." The metal legs of her chair scraped along the floor as her eyes flashed fury at him. "You know, I'm beginning to see you were right. You *are* a heartless bastard when things don't go your way. Maybe I've had a narrow escape from—"

He grabbed her wrist when she pushed off from her chair. The idea of her going off with a man he loathed was twisting him up inside out. But it was no reason to take it out on her. "I'm sorry, Nush. I have no excuse."

She stared down at him, her chest rising and falling, her usually mobile mouth pinched. Slowly, she nodded.

He should've let go of her then. Instead, he ran his fingers over her wrist, loving the wild thrum of her pulse underneath. He wanted her, he admitted to himself then, for himself. He wanted to act on it. He wanted to finish what she'd started that night and all the different filthy ways he wanted to finish it…if he told her, would she blush? Or would she, with her usual enthusiasm, tell him to get on with it?

Every muscle in him jumped at the acknowledgment. But he could find no way to rationalize acting on it. No way he couldn't hurt her in doing so. No way he could let her become such a big distraction—and that was what she would be—when he was so close to achieving his goal.

She pulled her hand away from his and stared down at her plate. "If not for the fact that Mira asked Yana and me to stay back for a few days to be with her—the first time she's asked anything for me and Yana ever," she added, "I'd have left three nights ago."

Shock pummeled him, punching his breath out of his chest. "Without even saying goodbye?"

Another shrug.

Caio decided to stop playing nice. To stop wondering the whys and whats of the inner workings of his twisted mind. Right now, all he knew was that he couldn't let Nush go off on some months-long holiday. Not until he could figure out a way to smooth this thing between them. No way was he simply giving her up just yet. "You and I signed a contract to deliver a model worth ten billion dollars in eight months. You also know that Rao's sudden death has set us back by weeks."

He paused, gathering every ounce of steely resolve he could muster. "If you leave now, I'll have the lawyers sue you."

Head jerking up, Nush glared at him. "You're bluffing. You wouldn't—"

"Try me, Princesa."

Frustration made her bang the glass against the table, spilling the orange juice all over. "Why are you doing this?"

"Why are you so determined to run away with a bunch of no-good jerks you couldn't stand to be around even as an impressionable teenager? You can't convince me that it's truly what you want."

Grabbing a napkin and wiping her fingers,

she sat back in her seat and studied the man in front of her.

Anger and something else made her itch for a fight. Outrage that he was playing dirty? A strange satisfaction that finally, finally, she was seeing the true Caio? A cocktail of emotions thrummed through her and she wanted to keep drinking it. Just when she'd finally accepted that the kiss was how far he would allow it to go.

She'd stayed in her grandfather's leather chair long after he'd left that night, arms tucked around her knees, fighting the urge to chase after him. Fighting the urge to get in his face and make him acknowledge that while she'd started a tender exploration, he was the one who'd turned it into a carnal caress. Telling herself that she didn't regret kissing him. Not for a moment. Not ever.

Even now, if she closed her eyes, she could remember the bite of his teeth on her lower lip, the tight grip of his fingers as he'd tilted her head back for better access, feel the echo of his growl reverberate through her limbs.

She'd kissed other men in search of that spark, to prove to her body and mind that it was habit, or comfort or some undefinable quality that pulled her toward Caio.

But even with his golden gaze burning holes through her composure and determination, steely arrogance etched onto his every feature about how this was going to play out, Nush knew things had changed between them and it sent a thrilling shiver through her.

She'd spent years studying every nuance in his face and she knew his tics. Her heart rabbited in her chest.

It was in the way his gaze had swept over her bare shoulders and legs when she'd walked toward him. In the way it lingered just a fraction of a second longer over her lips when she'd licked the jam. In the way he even sat now, stiff and tense, as if he was consciously containing his movements.

Whether he'd act on those baser instincts driving him…she couldn't take a bet.

She lifted her coffee cup and took a sip of the smooth brew, wanting to poke at his control. "Do you know that what you're doing is called cockblocking?"

His eyes came alive with a wicked, devilish intent that said he was ready to play. He kicked one leg out and leaned the other foot on top of the first knee in a move that spoke of pure dominance. "Is that why you're going on this trip with a bunch of brats? To chase cock?"

Her cheeks burned fiercely at hearing that word on his lips but she couldn't retreat. Not now, when it was finally on. "Did you think I'd bury myself in the lab and cry over your rejection? It's lust. And who knows? Maybe it's just a product of exposure and proximity and convenience. I have spent hours locked up with you in that lab. I'll just have to find a new channel for it."

Caio flicked at an imaginary speck of dust from his collar. "I have to tell you, *querida*, Peter doesn't have the greatest reputation in that department."

"Peter and you are not the only fish in the sea."

Anger tightened the rugged planes of his face. "So you just want to make a host of bad decisions, that you won't even truly enjoy, in the name of living it up? Run away from your commitments?"

Ire shot through her. "I'd never turn my back on contractual obligations. And it's not due for another year. I'll start work on it in six months. Get your piece ready, then we'll put it together on time."

"That borders on arrogance given that it's the most complex project you and I have ever taken on."

"Then it's your fault, isn't it? You taught me too well."

A glimmer of a smile appeared on his grave face. And for a second, he was the man she trusted the most in the entire world. "And you're the one who insisted that project planning team provide sufficient buffer period, Nush." Something glittered in those golden eyes. "You're intent on running away at the most critical juncture of OneTech's existence. You leave me no choice but to think it's because you've been denied what you think you want."

"That's where you're wrong. I know what I want."

"Throwing a tantrum when you can't have your way, I'd expect something like that of Yana. At least she doesn't pretend to be anything but who she is."

And just like that, he delivered a truth that Nush didn't want to face. She couldn't even say he was manipulating her because he was telling her nothing but the truth. "Don't, Caio."

"Don't what? Make you face reality? Tell you that I can't afford to walk away like you, Princesa? Or to act out like Yana. Or to hide from it all like Mira. I can't do whatever I please."

"You're as ruthless as people claim you are."

It was almost as if he was glad for the aggression between them. Glad that he didn't have to pussyfoot around her now that she'd openly attacked him. "You've seen nothing yet, Nush."

Then he pushed off from the table, dismissing her as he did any other employee who didn't please him. Showing her that opaque hardness, the ruthless will that could reduce someone to a quivering mess.

"I'll hate you if you force me to stay, Caio."

He stilled, his shoulders tense. Every line of his body radiating displeasure. "Then you prove my point, Nush. You're no more grown up now than you were when you fought Rao and me about your Mom being sent to a care home permanently, even knowing that you couldn't look after her daily. Than when you used me to fight your battles with Rao."

His words made shame burn through her, rooting her to the spot. Even the warmth of the sun felt harsh and judging on her face. He tucked a lock of hair behind her ear, drawing a response automatically and mocking it. "Run away if you must, Princesa. But let's at least agree that you're definitely not ready for anything with me."

CHAPTER FIVE

IT TOOK EVERYTHING Nush had in her to walk into Caio's office at OneTech towers a week later. More than she had in her, in fact, to not turn tail and run away when she saw not only both her sisters present but also the last person she wanted to see—Laura Huntington.

Out of the periphery of her vision, she saw Caio straighten in his leather chair. With the floor-to-ceiling glass walls behind him, sunlight bathed his broad frame in an outline she knew well, keeping his expression in the dark.

That's for the best, she told herself, moving across the vast office toward her sisters. She and Caio hadn't spoken or even looked at each other in the week since their confrontation. Mostly because she'd been licking her wounds in private, letting Mira and Yana take her out for shopping and lunch and a much-needed spa day.

In hindsight, it had been exactly what she'd needed to gain perspective. Especially after learning that, in a shocking turn of events, Thaata had left all of his stock in OneTech to her. Not Caio, even though he'd promised to facilitate the transfer.

That and her mom's sudden and fiercely lucid reminder that she hadn't raised a coward who tucked tail and ran away when things didn't go her way had finally made her face up to the truth. But knowing what she needed to do didn't make it exactly easy to…do.

Caio saw her as a girl to be protected, as a naive, unworldly innocent because that was how she'd chosen to act, how she'd chosen to conduct her life.

No more.

Thaata had intended for her to head OneTech alongside Caio. That much had become clear from the fact that she'd inherited all of his stock in OneTech and not Mira or Yana.

She wasn't going to let Laura or her family railroad Caio into a partnership he didn't want, just for OneTech's sake. He'd done enough for them. Enough of him thinking OneTech's legacy and even Nush herself were his responsibilities to be protected at any cost.

It was time to grow up.

Yes, because your proposal is completely without any selfish motives, a voice whispered.

"I want to talk to Caio. Alone," she announced

loudly before her determination deserted her and she retreated into sterile safety.

Both Mira and Yana looked shocked enough that Nush knew this was the right thing to do. She'd been passive and inert and living her life in her own head for too long. Her sisters' expressions were full of a confidence that Nush embraced like a childhood blanket as they left.

"If it's about saving OneTech from the hostile takeover my father's planning," Laura offered, "I should stay."

"Actually it's up to me now," Nush managed through a dry throat.

She didn't miss how Caio straightened from his chair, how his gaze focused on her face with that laser-like intense focus. Arms folded, Laura looked to Caio for direction.

Nush exhaled, fighting the thread of anger weaving through her. It wasn't Laura's fault that she dismissed Nush, was it? She'd always preferred to leave the boardroom politics to Caio and her grandfather. But enough was enough. "Leave us, Laura. Now."

Whatever she heard in her tone, Laura complied this time. Only when the double doors closed behind her did Nush face Caio.

He'd walked around his massive desk and leaned against it, legs crossed. Through sheer willpower, Nush stopped her gaze from drifting up and down his body.

Still, there was so much of him to see, to absorb. He'd always been an energy source she'd gravitated to. From the custom-made white dress shirt that lovingly spanned the breadth of his shoulders to the column of his corded neck visible with the buttons undone to his chest, to the edges of the tattoo peeking out. He'd long ago discarded the suit jacket and the tie, had clearly run his hand through his wavy hair a few times—in anger or frustration or both.

The impact of their gazes meeting was like a thump of a fist against her chest. A flicker of heat flashed in those golden-brown eyes as they swept over her and left just as soon. Like a shooting star. Leaving Nush to wonder if she'd imagined it because she wanted to see it.

She patted a hand over her midriff, searching for the right words, nervous and way too aware of her own skin. But she had to get used to this level of awareness constantly.

"I'm surprised to see you're still here."

Nush bristled even as she welcomed the taunt. She'd take his animosity, his anger, his challenges, even deal with his monstrous ego— *Hello, Caio's ego*—if it meant he wasn't coddling her. This was progress.

"Come to say a final goodbye?"

"That would make you happy, wouldn't it? Then you can just dismiss me as…" Nush closed her eyes and fought to take a deep breath.

When she looked back at him, those golden eyes regarded her thoughtfully.

"I've decided to put off my…break for the time being. A few weeks probably. Until my new plan takes care of every problem."

Fury raced across his features before he schooled his features back into that impenetrable mask he showed everyone. "And may I ask why the sudden change of heart?" Something sinuous trickled through the air between them. "Please don't tell me there's truth to the rumors of alliance…" he spat it like the word was distasteful on his tongue, "between you and him?"

"You're the one who's obsessed with the idea of him and me, Caio. You and his father."

"So you aren't marrying that idiot then?" Caio asked, his face still set in taut lines, no glimmer of humor in his eyes.

Nush walked to the sitting area and poured herself a glass of water, her heart thundering at how close he came to the heart of the matter. "God, no," she said over her shoulder before drinking it all in one go.

She'd barely put the glass down when he stood before her, taking up personal space, sending her pulse flying.

"Then why have you been spending the last few days at his penthouse with his gang of useless deadbeats? Did you know that Peter Huntington Sr. has been going around insinuating that an engagement announcement is imminent? That your…" his upper lip lifted in obvious disgust, "union is the new direction that OneTech needs desperately."

It took some serious facial gymnastics to keep the satisfied smile that wanted to bloom off her face.

Maybe she was going about this the wrong way. Maybe putting her feelings out there every time Caio demanded wasn't the way to go. And maybe…just maybe a little petty revenge wasn't quite out of her reach.

"What I was doing with Peter is none of your business now, is it? As to his father, I'd think you'd know better than to believe anything the man says. He's always tried to cause a rift between you and Thaata. Now he's playing the same games with you and me."

Caio flicked at his cuffs and Nush knew it was to hide his relief. "For a woman who keeps changing her mind every two hours, you seem to be very aware of everyone else's motivations."

"Don't get used to it," she said on a sigh. "I'm only playing along until things settle down. Until I get what I want."

"Which is what exactly, Anushka? A week ago, you couldn't wait to get far away from… here," he said, using her own words.

"I'm allowed to change my mind, aren't I?"

"Why though?"

"Because you were right. I was running away from…a lot of things. And that's not the kind of person Thaata hoped I'd be. And you, your actions, your rejection… I can't let it define me either."

A low, soft curse escaped him. "I didn't reject you. I—"

"Let's not get into semantics, shall we?" She added a casual shrug. Maybe this was the way to get over this ridiculous attraction—to pretend that she was over it. If she did it long enough, she'd start to believe it too. "The fact is I'm not going anywhere right now. And I have a solution to keep OneTech in your hands."

A muscle jumped in Caio's cheek. Tension radiated from him as he ran a hand over his jaw. And for the first time in days, Nush felt like she was finally standing on hard ground.

"Unless…" She couldn't help adding, "You're the one with the problem now?"

"What the hell does that mean?"

"You don't look happy to see me, Caio. If it's going to be this hard for you to be around me, then I'm not sure my plan has a chance of—"

He pushed off the desk with such lethal elegance that Nush had to force herself to stay still and not step back. Stopping just close enough for her to breathe in the scent of him, to feel the heat of his body, now familiar in a different way, hit hers, unspooling that wanton need in her lower belly. Those enigmatic eyes studied her, flicking from her eyes to her nose to her mouth and then back up. "I didn't realize you were capable of playing games, Princesa." Pure challenge dripped in every single word. "Especially with me."

Two more steps and she could press her chest against his. Two more steps and she could learn if he was affected by her proximity at all. Two more steps and…

She shrugged again, and wondered if it would become a tic she couldn't control soon. "I'm just making sure you're okay with my presence, Caio. It's imperative that we get along, despite our…*differences*, if you want me to save One-Tech."

"Save OneTech? Then why didn't you attend the board meeting this morning?" His mouth flattened. "I could've used your support there—seeing as you now own all of Rao's stock."

The bitter twist of his lips made her forget all her anger with him. "Are you angry with Thaata?"

He took in a deep breath. "I don't know if I should admit it to you, Nush."

Nush gripped his wrist, realizing how close they stood until he stilled. "Whatever else has occurred between us, or not occurred," she said, "I'd never turn against you, Caio. Do you think he just forgot after Nanamma's loss?"

"No," Caio said, surprising her. "Rao had a mind like a steel trap. He didn't forget anything. He left you everything knowing full well what he was doing. Knowing I'd resent him for it."

Surprised, Nush stared at him. "But why?"

Caio shrugged. And Nush had a feeling he knew. But he would never tell her. And really, she had no interest in knowing what the ongoing battle between him and Thaata had been about. She didn't need any more headaches.

"Whatever Thaata's reason, he must have underestimated my intense dislike for boardroom backstabbing *and* my loyalty toward you."

It was Caio's turn to look shocked. But he didn't let her linger on it by moving toward her, his gaze as impenetrable as ever. "You're still loyal to me after everything that happened, Princesa?"

"Of course I am," Nush said, trying to make light of the matter. "That's what being an adult is actually about, isn't it? Putting aside personal differences and doing the right thing for everyone? I've never doubted that OneTech belongs in your hands. And thankfully, I've figured out a way to make that happen."

His gaze searched hers, a vertical line appearing between his thick brows. Her fingers tingled at her side, itching to press at that ridge he got when he was thinking, wanting to smooth it away. "How?"

"We'll marry. I can sign over my stock to you, you'll be the majority stakeholder, even more than before, and I can go back to my lab."

"No. Absolutely not," Caio said in a soft voice even as the idea took wings in his head and began fluttering at a speed that he couldn't contain.

Nush would be his wife. He wouldn't have to worry about her or how to protect her from fortune hunters and their clutches now that she was even wealthier.

Rao's vision for OneTech would be preserved.

Peter Huntington Sr.'s grubby, greedy hands could be kept off the company.

Nush was ready finally, clearly, to step in and take a bigger role at the helm of OneTech, as Rao had always wanted.

Whatever Rao had thought to thwart Caio from would again become a distinct possibility as the CEO of OneTech.

Her idea was perfect in every which way, took care of every eventuality. In theory, it was the best solution.

He would pay millions more than the stock was actually worth—he wouldn't undercut her in any way. All he'd need to do was sign a piece of paper that legally bound her to him.

The reality was a leap of a universe away. She'd be his wife. In every way that could mean. The woman he hadn't been able to stop thinking of kissing would be his wife. Would have his deepest commitment. Because for all that Rao had called him cynical, Caio had always believed that marriage was a beautiful bond between people who gave it trust and love. Papa and Mama had shared a marriage like that.

Rao and his wife had shared a commitment like that.

And while he'd never seen it in his future after the mistakes he'd made by falling for his stepbrother's intended, a commitment to Nush would be different.

And his imagination and his libido ran little circles in his head, already breaking any rules he might want to put in place.

"No."

With a long exhale, as if he was nothing but an irritable child throwing a tantrum, Nush simply ignored his outburst, picked up the watering can, filled it at the attached en suite and began watering the plants on the ledge.

Plants she'd added to his office almost two years ago after calling it "a sterile, ugly box made of glass and chrome and leather" that might permanently damage his mental balance. As he'd discovered in the last few days, while stewing in jealousy and protectiveness and something else that he didn't want to think of, there was no erasing Nush from his life.

Wherever he turned, every nook and corner of his personal life he examined over the last decade, she was present. With her laughter, with her genius, with her awkwardness, with her grief, she'd etched herself into the fabric of his life.

And if she were to become his wife too…he'd end up hurting her. Shattering her.

But Caio also knew that he had no good reason to say no to her proposal. Not unless he was also ready to admit that he hadn't been able to stop thinking of their kiss.

It had taken him every ounce of willpower he had to not check on her in the last week. To not go rushing in like some possessive, protective male on steroids and drag her far away from Peter's influence. To not demand that she should know her worth better.

Instead, he'd acknowledged—how mature

and self-aware of him—that it was time to let go. Both for his sake and hers. Time for her to make her own decisions—even bad ones—even though she'd clung to him when he'd kissed her, even though she'd declared that she'd wanted him for months. He'd even told himself that he'd been right to think it nothing but an infatuation borne out of grief and loss.

The last thing he'd expected was that she'd be back, full of that verve, those big eyes staring him down, armed with an idea that could change things for the better. Or worse.

Sunlight streaming through the glass walls outlined her body, as if just for his pleasure. For the first time since she'd walked in, Caio allowed himself to take her in completely, take in the differences in her that he hadn't been able to stop cataloguing. It was a losing battle anyway.

The white dress shirt stretched tight across her chest and shoulders, and the dark skinny jeans she'd tucked into only reminded him of those legs bare, long muscles glinting. Her hair had been subdued into two braids and the glasses were back on. She looked chic and sexy and stylish in a way that didn't conform to any standards set by others.

It was all Anushka Reddy—genius coder, socially awkward with a dirty mouth and a sensuous appeal that hit one like a punch to the solar plexus.

And the thin tie, multicolored and with lines of code all over, dangling innocently between her breasts… Cristo, one look at her and all he'd wanted to do was undo that tie, wrap his fingers around it to pull her closer, to slip his fingers under that shirt and…

"Caio, you're staring." She cleared her throat, ridding herself of that huskiness he wanted to hear again and again. "In a way that tells me you're imagining—"

"Jesus, Nush. Stop."

She ran a hand over the damned tie and then played with the edges of it. Her nails, painted a dark rust color, shone bright. Like her presence suddenly brightened his office. "Look, if we're going to be married, it's better to set things straight from the beginning, don't you think? I really don't want to pretend like we don't want to rip each other's clothes off and—"

His hand on her shoulder shut her up. Pink crested her cheeks but the daring minx held his gaze steadily. "If this is some kind of twisted game of petty revenge—"

"I wouldn't sink so low." Her chin dipped to her chest. "After Mira told me about the will and how…shocked you were, I realized what a god-awful mess I'd be leaving OneTech in if I left.

Drunk Peter let me know of his father's plans for the hostile takeover. I…couldn't sleep that night. To let Thaata's hard work and vision go to waste like that, to see the culture of the company change from what you and he built, the thought of all of those community programs canceled… all so the board members could pad their already fat pockets. It would be nothing but sheer cowardice. So I scheduled a call with Aristos and we went over everything—"

"You went to your sister's estranged husband?" That she had gone to Aristos instead of him incensed Caio.

"Yes. With Aristos, there are no preconceptions. He hears me, sees me."

"And I don't?"

A short laugh, full of scorn, escaped her lovely mouth. "We both know you don't. Or rather you have an outdated version of me in your head that you won't update. And it crashes the entire system."

Caio knew she was right, at least to an extent. He had a lot of preconceptions about her. About the role he wanted her to play in his life. About keeping her separate from the dirty politics of his everyday life. About not letting anything in the world hurt her…and yet, it was becoming clear that those very notions were hurting her.

That his refusal to accept her as she was now was hurting her.

"Does Mira know that you talked to him?" Caio asked, just to poke holes in her plan.

"No," Nush said with a roll of her eyes that said she saw through his cheap tricks. "It's got nothing to do with her, or you."

"Why him?" Caio couldn't help but admire her. She had covered all her bases, had thought of every possibility.

"Aristos has always been kind to me and he's an internationally renowned corporate lawyer and someone I could trust and—"

"I have a hard time believing he told you to marry me."

"No. He helped me understand how things stand. After this, I can go back to being—"

"Being my worker droid, you mean," he said, feeling the sting afresh all over again. At least, Nush had the grace to look ashamed.

"Something like that."

"You know, the number of times that comes up, I'm beginning to believe you truly think that I exploit your brain for personal gain. For the record, I resent that."

"I was angry when I said that. I'm over it now. For you to use me would mean that you have to first see me as your equal, right? It would be an actual development in our stilted relationship. I'm realizing you've a very twisted set of values."

"Nush…"

"Please, I can't spend another minute explaining to you that it's not abnormal or wrong or dirty somehow for me to want you. I'm twenty-three years old and yes, you're fourteen years older than me, but it's not like you're my father or cousin or…anything even remotely bordering on *ewww*." Her chest rose and fell with her agitation. "Although now that it's become clear how you see me, I'm half over it already. There's nothing more pathetic than lusting after a man who thinks you're a little girl who needs his protection."

She was more woman than any he'd ever met, Caio wanted to say. There was anger and determination in her, but there was also fear and something else he couldn't put his finger on. And yet, she was here. She'd taken the risk of approaching him with an idea despite the risk of his rejection again.

He held off all the words that rose to his lips, refusing to let his emotions drive him. He'd already done that once. He hadn't been cruel on purpose, but he'd been hard on her.

Arms folded at his chest, he watched her—her fire, her mobile mouth, her disillusion with him.

A part of him wanted to believe that her infatuation with him had truly passed. A part of him wanted to prove the opposite—with his mouth and hands and body—that she wasn't over him. For the first time in almost two decades, his mind and his heart seemed to be going in opposite directions. Leaving him irritable and tense, distracting him from his goal.

And now her outrageous idea that they should marry…the greedy, grabby part of him said she was the most valuable possession he'd ever possessed, urged him to accept the proposition. For now, at least.

He hadn't asked her for her help.

And yet, what if he hurt her tender feelings for him? Would he be able to face himself if he took advantage of her?

"I can see that you've put a lot of thought into this," he said slowly, fighting for reason amidst two conflicting parts of himself, "but—"

"A lot of thought?" Nush snorted. "I've spent a week talking to people I don't like, hanging out with Peter and his deadbeat friends listening to them talk about women as if they were dogs or horses, a day listening to my father bitch about Thaata and Nanamma and how they cheated him out of his rights and then I went to see Mama and she was in a *mood*. You can't believe I did any of it on a sudden whim."

She settled onto the couch, and stretched her long legs out in front of her, her chin dropping to her chest. "I'm all peopled out, Caio. Probably for the next decade." A long exhale shuddered out of her. "I don't know what Thaata was thinking leaving me all that stock. They're all piranhas and sharks and vultures and… I can even see why you have to be so ruthless day in, day out."

She'd sat in that very couch so many times over the years, come to him with some problem and asked for his help. And she'd always looked at him with such trust that Caio had felt like a hero. As if she was a conduit for him to make himself feel better.

Which was problematic in itself.

"Your idea, I'll admit, has merit," he said carefully, testing out the words on his tongue. "It solves our problems in a very comprehensive way."

Fingers laced at her neck pulled her shirt tightly across her torso as Nush studied him from under her lashes. "You wouldn't have sounded like it was a death sentence if it was Mira or even Yana proposing this…arrangement. I mean, you even dated Yana at Nanamma's urging. Why is it such a leap for you when all along Thaata wanted you to marry into the family? We both know that if Mira hadn't eloped with Aristos over a weekend, she'd have been suggested to you next."

A sliver of hurt in her words made him cautious with his own. "It's not a death sentence, Nush," he said looking down at her. "I already admitted that it's a good idea."

"But? You're not already married, are you? Because, Jesus, that could be horrible on so many—"

"Of course I'm not married."

Color high in her cheeks, she shrugged. "Well, it's not that much of a leap seeing none of us know much about you."

"I want to make sure you're not walking into this with any sort of…expectations."

"The fact that I'm here, further entangling our lives when I want to be nowhere near you, is only because I decided it's time to take responsibility for OneTech. For Thaata's legacy. Now, please, let's talk logistics. Then we can go back to avoiding each other."

"Is that what you were doing?"

"Prenup," she said, ignoring his question, counting out on her fingers. "How long we have to put up this charade for. What our statement to the media looks like. And, oh, yeah…"

"Prenup?" he said, more than surprised that she'd truly thought of everything.

"Yes. I went back to Aristos with my idea and he stressed that I get one."

"Because you can't trust me?"

"Oh, his first piece of advice was that my idea was a garbage fire. That I should stay far away from you. But then he also said that in a professional capability, you'd be the only man he'd trust, even before his own family."

"You have to know that I'd never—"

"That you'd never…ruin me financially. Yes, I know that. We're all very mature people here, with honor and integrity coming out of our asses. Honestly, all I want on the prenup is that if you cheat on me, I can sue your ass for everything you have."

"Cheat on you, Nush?" he said, her blood-thirstiness knotting his stomach tight with a hunger like he'd never known before. "That implies a prior commitment. Is this more than a simple marriage bargain on paper?"

"Yes. No." Her cheeks reddened. "I don't care if you think I'm not sophisticated enough for you to screw, Caio. But I draw the line at the world seeing you parade your long lineup of girlfriends while you're married to me. So yes, I want your commitment to not making me look like a fool in front of the world. Apparently, there's only so much my pride can take."

"And you, Nush? Will you promise the same? Will you stop chasing—"

"Yes, of course," she said, blowing at her bangs. "That's why we need to put a time limit on this. The celibate life is *not* for me."

"I wouldn't think so, given the number of dates you've been on in just the past year," he added drily.

"I hope you appreciate the sacrifice I'm making for the good of the company...blah, blah, Caio. All this adulting is exhausting." A glint in her eye caught his attention as she studied her nails. "I've completely accepted the possibility that the only two candidates that might bring me pleasure are this pink vibrator Yana gave me last year for my birthday or you."

Instant heat gripped him, a fist around his cock, making his skin hum. She was taunting him. He knew that. She was going to continue taunting him for however long they stayed married. Still, he couldn't beat away all the images her words conjured. Couldn't think of a better torment.

"Which reminds me," she said, and texted rapidly on her cell phone. "Yana promised to get me the latest model. Might as well stock up."

"Is that your plan then? To seduce me?"

"I guess that means you don't assume I hatched this whole plan to have you?"

He laughed at the idea and then sobered when he saw the very real apprehension in her eyes. Grabbing her hand, which he'd done a thousand times before, Caio squeezed it. "If it were Yana, maybe yes. But you're far too straightforward for such a conniving plan."

"Thank the universe for small mercies." Her throat moved on a swallow, and she plucked her hand from his. "I won't let everything Thaata worked for get destroyed because of my insecurities." Grabbing the oversized jacket she'd discarded, she slipped it on. "As for seducing you, I wouldn't know where to begin. But let's say that I do have high hopes for this fake marriage."

"Ahh." Suddenly, the idea of Nush trying to seduce him sounded like a fantasy he hadn't known he'd want. "What are those hopes?"

"Either we'll have sex and I can work you out of my system—because all the fantasies I've spun about how good it will be can't be real." Her throat moved down on a hard swallow. "Or we don't have sex but I realize what a controlling, arrogant, emotionally cold man you are and, hello…sweet liberation from two years of unrequited lust."

Two years? She'd wanted him for two years? Not just months. Which meant she'd dated all those men for what?

Caio rubbed a hand over his face. If he'd

needed any more proof that he didn't really know Nush, here it was. Not once, by gesture or look, had she let on that she was attracted to him. Not once had she acted differently with him.

"Why didn't you tell me?" The question escaped his lips despite his resolution to not dwell on this giant elephant that populated their relationship now.

"It's attraction, Caio. Desire. Lust. And this marriage…it's just an amendment to our partnership, isn't it? Like the one you suggested all those years ago. And when it's over, I can move on with my life. Without you in it."

She left without waiting for his assent. Because it was a given. They had no other choice.

He had no other choice. Not if he wanted to buy his stepfather's company and break it off for parts. Not if he wanted to look him in the eyes and let the abusive bully see his destruction in Caio's eyes.

Running a hand through his hair, he paced the length of his office, feeling like a caged tiger. For the first time in almost two decades, he felt like he'd been sucker punched.

He'd been angry with Rao for leaving all of his stock to Nush, for making her a target for both fortune hunters and the likes of Peter Huntington Sr., sharks already circling fresh blood. For leaving Caio with a god-awful mess instead of signing the papers that transferred his stock to Caio.

And yet, was this what his mentor had intended? For all he'd been a man of integrity, he'd played games like a maestro. Had Rao foreseen all along that Caio would be pushed to such lengths to protect both OneTech and even more importantly Nush? Or had he thought only to thwart what he'd called Caio's corrosive, self-destructive need for revenge, even from beyond the grave?

And yet, Nush had delivered everything Caio needed straight into his hands. Along with herself.

In his wildest dreams, he hadn't imagined that he'd be left with no other choice but to marry Nush. Or that every muscle in him would curl with anticipation.

Or most unthinkable of all—that the idea of marriage to the one woman who'd always brought out the best in him would fill him with a desperate need to make their arrangement permanent *and* real.

CHAPTER SIX

NUSH STARED AT the beautiful diamond ring set in a princess setting and a simple platinum band, a boulder a hundred times the size of the twinkling diamond lodging in her throat.

If only the ring had been big and garish...

If only she hadn't described the exact same style to Yana once at a jewelry store, which meant Caio had asked Yana what she'd like...

If only she hadn't wished, with all the fervent hope of a fourteen-year-old, that she'd find a man exactly like Caio to marry one day...

If only she hadn't let Yana persuade her to dress in a knee-length, ivory-colored sheath dress that made her look too much like a blushing, hopeful bride...

If only she hadn't let Mira convince her to have the ceremony in the backyard of her grandparents' house, just in case her mama wanted to attend.

If only Mama had stuck to her obstinate, hardheaded will and refused to attend.

If only all of them hadn't been convinced that they had to at least make it look real and romantic with Peter Huntington Sr. spreading vile rumors about Caio's supposed dark, wicked seduction of poor, innocent lamb that was her—because God forbid she could think for herself…

If only Caio hadn't worn a black suit that made him look like her every fantasy come true…

If only she wasn't a naive, impressionable, sorry idiot whose heart took dangerous flight when he stared at her with a thoughtful glint in his eyes when she arrived to stand by him…

If only her skin didn't tingle every time he touched her even innocently…

If only she'd realized that sneaky universe granted your wishes if you weren't careful—but not in the way you'd hoped for…

If only she hadn't acted on her desire and kissed him and didn't have to live with knowing how he tasted against her lips…

So many *if onlys* that should've stopped the fake ceremony from becoming all too real.

Until the moment when Caio had slid the ring onto her finger, she hadn't pondered too much on how the moment would land. How many real dreams she'd woven around finding that special someone who'd always want her, love her, need her in return. How much she didn't want to end up like her mom—angry and distant with a brittle self-sufficiency that had never served her or Nush well. How much shifting Caio into this new role in her mind and in her life made her feel anchorless, all of a sudden. How much of a raw, vulnerable and tangled mess a simple kiss could make of everything.

Was that her fate? To always want people in her life who in turn wanted to never let her in? To be abandoned by anyone she got attached to?

God, now she was feeling sorry for herself, and that was something she truly hated.

No, she couldn't let it go to her head or her heart. She had to stop giving away pieces of herself to Caio.

This arrangement of theirs had a shelf life.

After an hour of a placid, vacant smile, her cheeks hurt. Her scalp hurt from the complicated knot Yana had twisted her hair into and her feet hurt in the four-inch stilettos that she wasn't used to. And more than anything, her heart hurt—raged at the understanding grimace/smile Laura Huntington had cast Caio.

Commiserating with him over the big sacrifice he'd made by saddling himself with an unwanted bride, all for the good of OneTech.

It didn't matter that it had been Nush's own plan. That she'd seen the satisfaction in Caio's eyes when everything had been signed and transferred, that she needn't worry about the vision Thaata had held for the company.

With one pitying look, Laura reminded Nush that for Caio this was an unwanted wedding. An arrangement he'd been cornered into by circumstances. And it was the hard reminder Nush very much needed.

By seven in the evening, Caio had been locked up in his study with a team of lawyers and the executive team of OneTech—Laura included. Yana had kissed her on the cheek before she'd disappeared. Nush ended up dancing and chatting endlessly with Peter Jr. of all people, who seemed to have decided she needed looking after while her new husband ignored her.

After seeing her mom safely into the chauffeured car, she'd had enough.

The changes she'd wanted to make in her life didn't have to stop at owning her responsibilities with OneTech. Fake marriage or not, her life was still hers to live. Clinging to Caio for the few crumbs of his attention would only bring her back to square one.

Caio was knocking on Anushka's closed bedroom door when Mira found him. Her calm, placid gaze flicked to the dark violet velvet box in his hands and then back to his face.

"Where is she?" he said softly. Agitation

thrummed through him after he'd spent three quarters of an hour looking for Nush.

Mira shook her head.

When he glared, she sighed. "I only know she wanted to get out of here."

Caio waited, knowing that Mira had more to say. Out of the three sisters, Mira was the one he understood best, the one who was the most like him. She'd gone through a lot as a child, with a mother who'd abandoned her and an alcoholic father who left her to his parents to be raised.

Mira understood responsibility, duty and that some wounds would never heal. All you could do was to make sure the poison didn't seep out and ruin the people around. It was guiding his behavior with Nush.

But the damned woman challenged every one of his good intentions. He'd planned for them to have dinner with some of his closest associates, to show her his appreciation for helping him achieve his life's goal, though she was unaware of it. He'd planned to spend the evening with her. Only when he'd emerged from his meeting, Nush had disappeared.

Did she think her responsibilities to OneTech, to him, ended with her signature? He hadn't missed the smirk on Peter Sr.'s face when he'd failed to locate his "wayward bride," in the older man's words. The older man was already spreading the vile rumor that Caio had taken advantage of the poor, clueless Reddy heiress. And that it was far too close to the truth grated on him like nothing else had ever done.

"Mira?" he prompted with little patience.

"I'm betraying my sister's confidence by discussing her with you."

"Anushka has no secrets from me," he said, wanting it to be true more than it really was.

"Yana said something happened between you. Did she tell you then?"

Now it was Caio who felt as if he was betraying the woman he'd spoken vows to this morning.

They should have been simply words. Meaningless. Trite. Even taunting. Instead he'd found a strange solemnity to them as he looked at the woman who had always given him her trust, whether he'd deserved it or not. Who'd always looked at him as if he were a sunbeam that had brightened her day. Who reminded him of the man Papa had hoped Caio would be one day. That look in her eyes was an addiction he couldn't shake.

She'd looked achingly beautiful, and yet out of place in a dress and makeup she never wore. And when he'd seen her distress, her eyes widening at the profound gravity of the ceremony, he'd felt that conflicting war within himself.

He wanted to give Nush the world—answer the desire he'd felt in her trembling form when he'd kissed her cheek—and he also wanted to protect her from himself.

Damn it, what the hell did he want? Why was he so upset that she'd abandoned him an hour after their wedding?

"I think the whole ceremony…the way it went down…freaked her out. Then there was Laura Huntington."

Caio frowned. "What didn't she like? And what about Laura?"

"You have such a razor-sharp brain when it comes to business and politics, but you are just as dense as any other man when it comes to women. I thought you knew Nush better."

She was upset that Laura was there. Caio repeated the words to himself. Because she thought Laura and he were together? Because she'd assumed he couldn't do without Laura even for an evening? Because they'd been buried in his study for hours straight after the short ceremony?

"I needed Laura there. There was something I needed to push through the board before I…" He stopped, knowing that he was explaining himself to the wrong woman. "So she disappears instead of asking me about it? And she says the way I see her is outdated."

"Did you expect her to make a scene?" An uncharacteristic hardness twisted Mira's mouth. "Nush never pushes, never demands anything of others, is too happy to push herself into a corner in someone's life, content to be there. She spends hours waiting outside of her mom's room at that home every weekend hoping she'll see her, wanting her to know she's there. She keeps bringing Dad home after one of his episodes, begs him to shower, eat, looks after him as if he were a child for days after. She dropped the idea of going to college in New York in some stupid bargain with Thaata so that he wouldn't throw Yana out of the house after she pulled another of her stunts."

"Of course Rao had manipulated her."

Mira let out a laugh "She'll fight you if you even say that. That's how unconditional her loyalty is. Thaata loved us but yes, you and I know he was also a master manipulator."

And yet, Nush had told him that she was attracted to him. She'd taken the risk of kissing him. She'd come back after he'd told her she wasn't grown up enough for him, to save the company.

He hadn't appreciated how far out of her comfort zone she'd gone. How much courage it must have taken to walk back into his office. For all of five seconds, he felt utterly inadequate to be the recipient of such…pure emotion, whatever it was.

A part of him flinched, wanted to run far from it.

He pushed a hand through his hair as another piece fell into place. "So Rao knew that she…" He couldn't put it into words. Suddenly, everything Nush had given him felt like a gift he didn't deserve.

"I think so. He probably also guessed that she'd come to your rescue." Mira rolled her eyes. "If he hadn't taken such a bad turn, I think he'd have had it stipulated in writing. Sort of purchased you for his precious princess."

He raised a brow, knowing that Mira was trying to get her own shots in. "And here I thought you were the sweetest Reddy sister, Mira."

She shrugged. "You know better now."

"I didn't know what conditions you agreed on for this…fake marriage, but I hope you remember Nush gives of herself unconditionally. Doesn't mean we all deserve it."

"Is that a warning, Mira?"

"I'm trying to appeal to the better part of you. Or maybe I know that I'm talking to a kindred soul. You and I don't know the weight of such… open trust and affection. Nor do we know how not to shatter it, Caio." Shadows swirled in her eyes. "If you care about her, at all, get this thing annulled as soon as possible."

"That's," he said with a smile trying to take the bite out of his words, every instinct and rational thought revolting against the idea of annulment, "between Nush and me. No one else."

Mira blinked. "She's the best of us all, Caio. Don't hurt her."

"Where did she go, Mira?"

"Yana mentioned something about a new nightclub."

And Caio knew who the nightclub belonged to. He bit back a curse as fierce jealousy stormed through him. Even as he knew Nush wouldn't do anything to break their…what was it between them? An arrangement? A deal? A bargain? And what did she get out of it? All the benefits in this marriage were his. And he didn't like the imbalance of that. Didn't like being in her debt one bit.

"How long are you planning for this fake marriage to last?" Mira asked, interrupting his thoughts.

"When are you going back to that husband of yours?" he taunted. "I hear he's been like a wounded beast ever since you left him. And Aristos's veneer of civility was thin enough to begin with."

"Touché," Mira said, as something like panic touched her eyes. "I… I'm going back tomorrow. To Athens. Wish me luck, won't you?"

On a sudden impulse, Caio gathered Mira to himself and hugged her petite frame. She was stiff in his arms for a few seconds before she sank into his embrace. "You'll be glad to know your estranged husband and you are on the same wavelength."

"What?" she asked, eyes wide and bright at the mere mention of Aristos. The stubborn Greek, who was as close a friend as Caio had

had in the last decade, had won a point in his eyes when he'd arrived as soon as he'd heard of Rao's death and supported Mira through the grief. Granted, he'd only stayed for two days, but after nine months of his wife leaving him with no reason or note, as Aristos had shared after a couple of drinks, Caio had thought it showed what the man was made of.

"Apparently, he vehemently warned Nush against this marriage too."

She laughed then, and Caio thought there was both joy and grief in the sound. He squeezed her slender shoulders, realizing only in that moment how she and Yana had carved themselves a place in his cold, cold heart. They'd fought with him, challenged him, forced him to earn a place in their family and then steadied him with the kind of trust and affection that he'd been parched for, ever since Papa had passed away and his loss had changed Mama into a shadow of herself. But they'd never resented him for earning such a prominent place by Rao's side in OneTech and that was generosity Rao and his wife had taught all three of their granddaughters.

Caio sent another heartfelt thanks to the man who'd saved him all those years ago.

Maybe Rao had succeeded at his mission to chip away at his bitterness to a small extent, he thought. Or stopped the poison from spreading further and turning Caio into a toxic man in the very shape and shadow of the man he loathed.

Maybe there was a future ahead of him outside of the revenge he'd planned for so long. Or maybe he was buying into the romantic nonsense of today's ceremony. There was no way he could build ridiculous, far-fetched dreams around a woman who deserved better than him. All he knew, all he planned for his future was destroying someone else.

"Will you tell Nush I said goodbye?" Mira said into the comfortable silence. "I'm leaving first thing in the morning. I don't want her to think I abandoned her."

Caio nodded. "I hope you know that you're not alone, Mira, even if Rao's gone. If you need anything—"

"Ahh…but you and I both know that in some aspects of life, we are alone, Caio. It's written into our DNA."

"What's the point then?" he asked, feeling an intense vulnerability he hadn't known still lingered.

"The point is that there's always choices, Caio. I'm making a choice to return to Aristos, even though…" She sighed. With a familiarity that made him smile, she tapped his cheek with her fingers and smiled. "Let's hope we don't mess this up."

Caio pressed a kiss to her head and left to find Nush.

CHAPTER SEVEN

It took him two and a half hours to find Nush.

She hadn't been at Peter Jr.'s nightclub. Or rather it had been a short stop in apparently a long night of chasing entertainment like some college kid off on a night's rampage.

She's no older than a college kid, a voice whispered and he cursed. Neither had she been exaggerating when she'd argued that she'd buried herself in that lab for more than a decade. Just as he'd buried himself in acquisitions and mergers that would bring him closer to his goal. Their innate nature as loners had become the foundation of their relationship.

He'd had to track down Yana and threaten her—which wasn't an easy feat since nothing and no one could really control the volatile middle Reddy sister—and get Nush's location out of her. Even that was only after she'd received a text from Nush that she'd needed help.

So here he was, outside of a luxury hotel, still

chasing her. Solar lights placed along the huge courtyard punctured the bitter darkness of pre-dawn. He'd taken no more than two steps when he saw her and stilled.

Patchy moonlight glinted along her neck and her chest as she walked through the double doors, her gait slow. She came to a halt below the entrance archway. Her hair was still in that complicated knot, but she'd changed out of the wedding dress into a black leather skirt that skimmed her knees and a ribbed white skintight top that hugged every inch of her small breasts. A white dress shirt—her signature item —flapped over her shoulders. He followed the line of her long, long legs to find her feet encased in glittery pink high-top sneakers that brought an unexpected smile to his lips.

His chest loosened, relief spreading through him. This was the Nush he knew, the girl who'd always made him laugh, the girl who'd been a bright spot in his dark, revenge-obsessed thoughts.

And yet, she wasn't just that girl anymore either.

This was a woman who'd boldly told him how much she wanted him, who'd marched into his office with a solution. This was a Nush he wanted to know more of, a woman he could see himself... With a sigh, he cut off the direction his thoughts were going in too often.

Drawing closer, Caio noted that she held her bent arm close to her chest. Then the sling wound around her neck. "What happened, Princesa?"

She stiffened, her eyes huge and wide behind the thick glasses. "Caio..." She looked at her watch and then around herself. "What are you doing here?"

He touched his fingers to hers, and nodded at the cast around her wrist. "You're hurt. How?"

"Oh, there was a scuffle at the club. I slipped and broke my fall with my wrist. The X-ray showed a hairline fracture." She sighed. "It's been quite the eventful night."

"And day," he added.

"Hmm?"

"It was our wedding day, *querida*." He'd no idea why he felt the need to remind her of that. He was beginning to wonder if he knew right or wrong when it came to her.

She plucked her hand from his looking like a deer caught in headlights. "Did Yana send you? I'm sorry that you had to drive here at this time—"

"Yana didn't send me anywhere. I spent most of the night already looking for you. I don't like not knowing where you are."

She raised a brow, all outrage and bite. "Since when did I have to report to you?"

"Since always, Nush," he said, her temper egging his on. "Why didn't you call me?"

"I lost my phone."

"And yet, you called Yana."

"I don't remember your number."

His mouth twitched. "You're a horrible liar."

The bank of elevators behind them pinged. A familiar figure exited the glass car and every muscle in Caio's body tightened with such ferocious anger that he covered the little gap between him and Nush as if she were prey.

His new, albeit unplanned acquisition.
His wife.
His. In every way that mattered.

Cristo, he couldn't remember one good reason why he shouldn't think of her as his, why he shouldn't welcome this fortune that had directly fallen into his lap.

Peter Jr. took one look at him and his steps faltered.

A palm landed on Caio's chest and his muscles clenched at the innocent contact. "Stop posturing around and intimidating Peter."

"It's not my fault if he's scared of me. He knows he shouldn't be sniffing around you."

"Jesus, he's not sniffing around me. And believe it or not, he was the only one who paid attention to me today." When Caio stared at her, she pointed to the cast.

"Apparently, away from his bullying father and his band of toxic peers, he isn't half-bad. He even apologized for… Anyway, we actually talked and laughed and danced… I enjoyed his company."

Mira's words came back to haunt Caio. God, Anushka *was* too soft for her own good. Too forgiving. "Your discovery is a little too late, Princesa. He can't have you."

"What?"

He tucked a wavy lock of hair that fluttered at her jaw, taunting him. "I said he can't have you." Caio softened his own voice. "You're mine, Nush."

"Either you're continuing with the theme of mocking something that I consider sacred or you're an arrogant ass who doesn't want me but doesn't want anyone else to have me," she said, swaying on her feet, "and I—"

Caio steadied her. "You said we weren't even allowed to indulge in mild flirtations. I'm just reminding you of your own conditions."

Big, wide eyes considered him, exhaustion written into her features. "You could have just said that instead of issuing…possessive statements."

With Mira gone and Yana's unreliable and chaotic schedule, he didn't want to leave Nush alone at that big house. Which meant she was coming with him to Brazil tonight.

A huge part of him protested. He wanted to keep her separate from the poison in his life. Wanted to keep her away from all his bitterness. Wanted to keep his own image untarnished in her mind. But it wasn't an available choice anymore.

Anticipation coiled through him even as he acknowledged he had quite a fight on his hands. "Are you in pain?"

She pushed the bridge of her glasses up her nose and nodded. "I don't think the pills have taken yet. Especially not enough to make me tolerate your territorial, jealous husband act."

When she stepped to his left, he got in her way, blocking her with his body. It was confrontational in a way he'd never addressed her before. But it didn't feel wrong either. Nothing felt wrong anymore. In fact, every filthy thought, every overwhelming urge, every spike of hot need pulsing through him felt deliciously, irrevocably right.

What the hell had those vows done to him?

When she signaled to Peter Jr, he appeared with an umbrella in hand, a small smile twisting his mouth.

Caio addressed the younger man. "Leave, Huntington."

Peter glanced in Nush's direction, mumbled something to himself, pretended as if he was considering standing up to Caio and then ran down the steps without a backward glance.

Mouth falling open, Nush stared at the fast-receding man. She slapped at Caio's abdomen with the back of her hand, her eyes round with anger. "He was my ride."

"You have me."

"Stop reminding me of those ridiculous rules. It's not like I was going to elope with him."

"I don't want you around him."

"You're a thug, Caio Oliveira," Nush said, turning to him, gaze pinning him. "A bully. An arrogant ass. And I don't need your pity. It's bad enough…"

"Bad enough what, Nush? What was so bad that you've been running from me all night?"

"I'm not running from anything. I smiled at that mockery of a ceremony. I ate cake and laughed about the silly jokes everyone made about how you've had to jump in and save the poor, plain, weird Reddy sister again. I signed every piece of paper you put in front of me. And when you told me to leave, I followed your order, without looking back, like a good little solider."

Her voice was full of an ache that he knew

he was the cause of. It terrified him like nothing else had ever done. Her lower lip wobbled before she bit down on it.

"You're acting like this was a real wedding day…"

"What would make it real then?"

His question vibrated in the air around them with all the intensity of a lightning strike. And suddenly, Caio wondered if it could be that simple. If that was what he'd been fighting against since she'd walked into his office and declared her outrageous proposal.

The idea of simply keeping Nush was a dangerous thought on so many levels and yet so alluringly appealing to the deepest core of desires and wants he'd buried under need for vengeance. Suddenly the sweet forbidden temptation that she was, was very much within reach. And he knew he wasn't going to be able to let go of her.

Not now.

Not ever.

"What are you saying?" Nush said in a whisper.

"What would it take from me to make it real? A promise of fidelity? My commitment to make this work? My word that I don't want anyone else? Only you." Lightning flashed across the sky as if to underscore the fierce resolve in his words. A tremor skittered across her shoulders.

"Ever since that kiss, all I've done is think of what else I'd do with you." She didn't say anything for so long that Caio felt a flicker of unfamiliar fear twist through his gut. "Come, Princess. You're in pain. We can discuss this later when—"

"You want this to be real? Our…" she stumbled over the word, "marriage? When did you decide that?"

Shedding his jacket, he draped it around her shoulders, careful to not jostle her wrist. "I see no reason why it can't be the real thing. Not when we both want each other, not when we're already tied to each other. Not when I know no other woman would give me the kind of…loyalty that you do. The ceremony we had, the dress, the cake, the guests, the ring…it spooked you because it felt too real, didn't it?"

Even in the little illumination, he could see the shock in her eyes. "Why did you go to such trouble?"

"I only plan to get married once, *querida*, and I thought it a fitting tribute to your grandparents' memory to have it at their house."

She pushed at him with an angry growl. "Don't play games with me, Caio. Please. This… what you're proposing, it can't have anything to do with Thaata or OneTech or anything else. It has to be about you and me. If not, if you're playing with my feelings for any other reason, then you're…you're a monster and I'd never forgive you."

Her gaze held his in a silent, soft challenge and yet her words struck him hard at his core. Mira's words came to him and he marveled at how well she knew Nush. If he got this wrong, if he ruined this between him and Nush, if he fractured her faith in him, it would shatter her and that in return would destroy him. At a level from which he'd never recover.

It was a risk with odds set high for failure because he could never give Nush all of himself. Parts of him had been lost long ago, to even himself.

And yet, the want in his gut persisted. The idea of leaving Nush behind as he watched the destruction he'd set in motion alone, thousands of miles away from her, felt empty. All his hard work and persistence and sacrifices, everything he'd denied himself in the pursuit of revenge… couldn't she be the respite he allowed himself? Wasn't he allowed to be selfish for once?

He knew her more than he did any other woman. He liked her company, he trusted her and damn it to hell, but he wanted to finish what she'd started in that study. He wanted to take her to his bed and keep her there until all she knew was him.

It was just a matter of making sure she knew what he could give and what he couldn't. And he'd begin with the truth. At least in this. "When I made the arrangements, it was to ward off filthy rumors that I was taking advantage of you. I wanted the board and the world to see that it was more than a convenient paper arrangement. That you and I share more."

"But we don't share anything more and it *is* nothing but a filthy, monetary transaction—that you kicked me out of that room before my signature dried is proof enough."

"I've been working toward a…time-sensitive acquisition for a long time," he said, hating that he'd already hurt her. "That paperwork needed to be signed and sealed before I left town."

"You turned the wedding into an empty mockery of the real thing when you know how much I… Maybe you were right that I don't really know the real you," she said in a defeated tone that sounded like a death knell. "Not two weeks ago, you told me we can't have that sort of relationship. You said it was the biggest mistake of your life to kiss me. So what's changed?"

Caio picked his words carefully. "Marriage is not some cheap, dirty affair, Nush. It's a commitment, bigger than anything I've ever made to anyone. Doesn't that say something?"

She searched his eyes. "You're not letting me

have you as some sort of medieval honor payment because I signed over my stock to you without a peep, are you?"

Hand under her chin, he tilted her face up, letting her see the desire he'd been fighting from the moment she'd touched her lips to his. "There's nothing honorable about what I want to do to you. Is that answer enough?" He didn't have to bend too much to speak at her ear and he loved that too. He loved that she fit so well against him, that she fit so well into his life. The shiver that wrecked her when their bodies grazed found an answering thrum in him. "As for who's going to have whom…we'll see about that, *querida*."

She licked her lips and he groaned. "And if it's horrible and boring and clunky…then what? You'll return me with a patched-up label and the deal's off?"

"Maybe," he said with a laugh.

She growled and punched him and called him names and he gathered her closer. Just one arm around her shoulders, without betraying the demanding tightness of his own body.

Only then did he realize that she was shaking. That she was nervous around him, that this bridge they were crossing to a new place in their relationship wasn't easy or simple or uncomplicated for her and that she'd still made the first move. That she'd thought this was worth exploring, worth being so honest about.

It was just his male ego that was flattered at her interest, he told himself and yet, the lie didn't stick. It was more. The dark, empty corner of his psyche being soothed.

"I consider marriage sacred. Not a game, not a bargain, not a show we put on for others. Not an experiment we try until we get bored."

"It's not any of those things for me either." He pressed his mouth to her temple, unwilling to wait another second for the taste of her skin. With his finger, he traced the arch of her neck and the pulse fluttering violently there. A soft gasp escaped her, turning him rock hard, but she still held herself stiff. "If it gets that bad, Nush, I'll let you dump me."

"You're an arrogant, conceited bastard," she said, looking up at him, "and I'm not—"

Suddenly, the sky opened in dense sheets of rain. In the breadth of a few seconds, they were both completely drenched.

Caio could no more stop looking than he could stop breathing as he gathered his jacket around her shoulders. The flimsy excuse for a top stuck to her skin, revealing the stiff points of her nipples.

Desire punched him, the pouring rain no match for the heat of his body. Caio bent and lifted Nush until she was safely tucked against his chest.

For all of thirty seconds, she was quiet, overtaken by shock, one arm clutched close to her chest. Then she was demanding to be put down, yelling that he was a caveman and that she wasn't fragile and how dare he…

Hefting her up in his arms, Caio pressed a rough, sudden kiss to her lips. Like a fierce summer storm that didn't last too long, her ferocity died and she clung to him, moaning, licking, kissing him back.

She tasted like cold rain and liquid desire, the tips of her fingers digging into his shoulder. He swallowed her moan of complaint as she tried to get deeper, delve closer. The depth of her desire for him, the explosiveness of her response left him shaking and his steps faltered as he wondered if he could keep her for a lifetime without letting her see all of him.

But he'd try, because the alternative of an empty future after he achieved his goal didn't bear thinking about.

CHAPTER EIGHT

NUSH LOOKED AROUND the luxury rear cabin of the private jet she'd been deposited into by a wet, thoroughly rumpled Caio.

She had no memory of the car ride except for snuggling up against the damp warmth of his body and the misery of being stuck in a bodysuit that clung to her skin like a wet rash and the constant pulse of pain radiating from her wrist.

She looked around the spacious cabin with its gleaming wood paneling and ultra-modern shower in the corner. The dark navy-colored duvet was soft against her fingers. She grimaced at the wet patch her rain-soaked clothes had immediately left on the bed and hopped away to sit on the single chair.

With her left arm tucked against her chest and the shoes wet and tight, trying to pull them off was a losing prospect. Except for a few unintended crunches for her ab muscles, she got no further. With a frustrated cry, she gave up. Instantly, thoughts rushed in like a tsunami.

A real marriage...to Caio.

A shiver ran down her spine and it had nothing to do with the dampness of her clothes. A lifelong commitment, a partnership and he would be hers...forever, in a way no one had ever been. She didn't miss how high-handed he was being, bringing her aboard his jet, assuming she'd happily go wherever he brought her. His sudden decision that it would be a permanent partnership.

The sheer arrogance of the man took her breath away. It was also the same decisiveness that made her feel all warm and gooey inside. Because Caio moved through life with a conviction, a commitment that never wavered once he gave it. And that he was promising it to her was a breath-stealing temptation, a fantasy coming true. Beneath all her affront and outrage at his executive decision, the woman in her, the romantic fool in her wanted to grasp it with everything she had.

But the little girl in her—the one who'd survived a chaotic childhood, the one who faced abandonment at every turn—was terrified that she'd lose him if they did this, that he'd abandon her too if she let herself have this.

You're mine, he'd declared with such raw, possessive intent that reminded her that there were facets of Caio she didn't know. That he carefully controlled what he did share.

How would a relationship ever work if he didn't even let her know him? If everything was based on logic and compatibility, or on the minimal facts that she was loyal and attracted to him? If he always controlled the reins of it?

Nushie, it doesn't have to be any different from the affair you proposed, that same voice whispered again and Nush grabbed it with both hands. A quiet determination stole through her.

If he truly wanted this to be a real thing, then he'd have to give her all of him. He'd have to prove it to her. Until then, she'd treat this as a temporary madness they were giving in to. That way, at least she wasn't leaving herself even more vulnerable to him.

"Are you kidnapping me?" she asked when Caio walked into the cabin a few minutes later. The question was nothing but token since they'd been airborne for a little while now. She also had no doubt that he'd changed his plan to accommodate her because of her broken wrist. Ugh, so much for starting off on an even footing.

"I'm taking you with me on a trip that's been on the schedule for a while," he said, without meeting her eyes.

What she'd thought a luxuriously expansive space just minutes ago shrunk with his broad frame in it. There was a strange tension to his frame as he moved around the cabin, grabbing things.

Was it because of their particular destination? Or because he was already finding her presence intrusive?

They'd share spaces like this on a daily basis—the bedroom, the kitchen, the bathroom, even a tub maybe. For days and months and years...*if* it worked out. They'd create their own traditions, make holiday memories, maybe even have kids. He'd be hers forever—unapologetically hers, irrevocably hers.

He wouldn't leave her for anything, wouldn't make her wonder if he'd break his word or send her off. As a mentor, friend and colleague, he'd been steadfast. As a husband, he'd be...

Jesus, Nushie, why don't you just prostrate yourself at his feet then? The caustic words sounding very much like Yana put a break on her spiral. It was wishful thinking, a fantasy she'd weaved.

He was secretive and arrogant and controlling, she reminded herself. And he thought her some kind of unicorn he had to protect.

God, she was going to lose it with such constant, conflicting thoughts.

"Because I can't be trusted to look after myself?" Her words came out full of distrust and fear.

"Because you're hurt and I don't want you fending for yourself alone in that big, empty house." He sighed, added as an afterthought, "And because I want you with me."

"Where are we going?"

"To an island I own off the Brazilian coast."

"Is that where your family lives?"

"They used to. Before…" his jaw clenched and released, "a long time ago."

Nush frowned. "Wait, this acquisition…does it have something to do with your family?" Because that would explain the lengths he'd gone to, wouldn't it?

Marrying her.

His barely hidden agitation as she'd signed the stock over.

The hours and hours of strategy planning with his executive team.

His furious determination to acquire the company despite Peter Sr.'s vicious protest that it was nothing but a liability unsuitable for OneTech.

"It's a long story to get into now, Princesa."

"We have a long flight ahead of us," she said, before leaning her head back and closing her eyes. "I'd like nothing but—"

"Here, let me."

Nush sighed as long fingers cleverly massaged

her temples and relieved the tension that had been building all day. She tucked away the fact that he hadn't answered her question, for now.

With a groan she couldn't suppress, she leaned her head forward until it hit his abdomen, begging for his fingers to go deeper and farther. He granted her unspoken request, his fingers kneading gently at her scalp and then back around. With her arm between them, Nush steadied herself with a hand on his stomach.

Tight, hard muscles clenched under her touch. She spread her hand around innocently enough, needing to touch more of him. A ripple of movement was her reward. Then she played with his belt buckle, the cold metal a nice break from the warmth suffusing her. A different kind of tension thrummed into life as she imagined sending her fingers on a southward quest. Her mouth dried at the thought of tracing his shape and length, of raking her fingernails over rock-hard thighs…

"I've asked the staff to bring you something to eat," he said, stepping back. Cutting the contact without pushing her away. "A shower, food and sleep."

She nodded without looking at him and fisted her hand that felt suddenly bereft. Damn, why had she hesitated?

"So docile, Princesa? You must be in a lot more pain that you're letting on."

She looked up to find him regarding her with a frown. "It's been a long day and I'm just gathering my thoughts. But I can't pin one down."

"Anything you want to share?"

Nush stared at him, wondering at how easily he turned it back to her. How he deflected her delving into his mind, his heart. Neither had he missed that her suddenly subdued temper meant something deeper was needling her. "It's not an easy jump to think of you as my…husband," she said, testing the shape and weight of the word on her tongue. "I've never even thought of marriage in my future." She didn't say it might have been because her present had been mostly obsessed with him.

"Which is why I'm not going to rush you into anything."

Anything like what? Sex? Was the damned man going to leave her hanging again? "You know that I grew up with Mama hating anything related to marriage. She thought it was nothing but an institution held up by men to control women."

"It does become that in certain circumstances, full of poison and control," he added in such a savage tone that she was shocked by it.

When he didn't elaborate, she said the first

thing that came to her mind. "I always wondered if she sometimes regretted not accepting when my dad proposed. Although seeing that he's incapable of anything but his commitment to alcohol, she made the right choice."

"He proposed to your mother?"

Nush nodded.

"Does it bother you that you...are illegitimate?" There was a fierce quality to the question as if the injustice of it bothered him.

"Not really. Being Mama's daughter meant understanding real-life matters at a very young age. And that I got to meet Thaata and everyone when I was four made me realize it didn't make a difference. Mira and Yana had nothing I didn't have. In fact, I was the one who had a mother that loved her. Even if sometimes, her mental health didn't make for the warmest, greatest upbringing."

"Your devotion to her is admirable."

Nush frowned at his question. But one look in his eyes told her he wasn't being contentious or dismissive, that he was even angry on her behalf.

"She could have easily handed me off to Thaata. It became clear that he asked her to, enough times. It would have made her life, her work, her moods...everything easier. She could have just visited me when she had time. But she didn't. She loved me, as much as possible for her, in whatever way her mind allowed. She tried her best and that's all I needed."

He stared at her with such stark, naked emotion that Nush looked away. It wasn't uncomfortable but it made her feel as if she'd suddenly bared all of herself to his gaze—every insecurity, every vulnerability—and he was rooting through it all.

Staring at her fingers, she struggled to bring back the topic to what plagued her. "She'd spent years brainwashing me to never give in to marriage and yet when I asked her if she wanted to attend the ceremony…she was beyond excited. I think it has something to do with you," she said, solving at least one puzzle.

Astonishment painted over his features. "What?"

"I think you're the one man who managed to win Mama over. She trusts you and…" Nush swallowed the hard lump of gratitude that lodged in her throat. "Thank you for always being kind to her, Caio. For always thinking of what's right for her, especially when I couldn't. I know that she felt threatened by Thaata to let him handle it."

"I didn't do it for your gratitude, Nush."

"Why did you?"

"Because she needed looking after. And so you'd be happy and settled and worry free. I told you before. You reminded me of myself at my most…powerless. And yet, you didn't…" he cleared his throat, "you don't let bitterness touch you. I'm arrogant enough to like it that I had a hand in keeping you like that. Untouched and innocent."

She scrunched her nose at that, not liking it one bit. Not liking it at all that he still saw her as some sort of fragile creature to be protected. "That makes me sound like fruit," she said, loathe to disturb the strange, tension-filled truce they seemed to have reached.

"Would it be better if I said fruit that is ripe and ready to be eaten?"

"You need work on your flirting. That sounds *ewww.*"

Sitting down on the bed in front of her, he pinned her with that weighty gaze. His thighs straddled hers and the thick, hard press of them caging her felt deliciously lethargic. "What's truly bothering you, Princesa?"

"You've never even had a girlfriend for more than a week. It's hard to believe that you're doing this because you…want to."

Arms folded, he seemed to consider his words. "Just because I didn't mention marriage doesn't mean I don't believe in it. I had other things occupying all my attention."

"Like this acquisition?" she poked again.

He sidestepped her yet again by giving her a morsel of something she was desperate for. "My parents had a great marriage built on trust and respect and an unshakeable foundation of… friendship."

She had a feeling he meant to say love but left it out on purpose. And she wasn't sure how she felt about that either. Did she want him to profess love to her?

God, no, came the instinctive, immediate answer.

She wouldn't believe him to begin with. Love never had anything to do with Caio's actions. He didn't even let anyone close. Even now, even when he was giving her this commitment, she had a feeling she wasn't going to get anything more than what they already had.

Whether a relationship between them could survive with his conditions and her fears was anybody's guess.

"We already have the foundation, Nush. A commitment is all that's needed. And I'm making that to you."

It should have sounded arrogant, like he was issuing a decree and expected her to fall in line. And it was that partly. But all Nush could focus on was the solemnity to his words and the overwhelming urge to set some kind of boundaries on her own expectations. Self-preservation was a bitch.

"Will you promise that you'll never lie to me? That you won't stay in this arrangement for some sort of twisted honor that dictates that you can't desert me? That you'll see me as an equal—not Rao's granddaughter or the woman who gave you OneTech or the girl you rescued a long time ago?"

"Yes, to the first and second. The third…it's not easy to separate you from all those things, Nush. And stop calling it an arrangement."

"I need time, Caio. I can't just jump in like you. I…"

"I want you heading OneTech with me. I want you in my bed, beneath me, giving this your everything."

A full body shudder overtook Nush as that very vivid image hit her.

When he grinned in response to her reaction, Nush decided she'd like nothing better than to unravel him too, bit by bit.

Whatever path this took, she'd at least solve the complex mystery of Caio. She'd learn every inch of him, inside out, until her fascination with him was gone, until there was no unknowns left between them.

In the meantime, she was simply going to enjoy the ride.

Thick towels in the same navy blue of the sheets, a first aid kit and something else was dumped onto the bed. And then Caio was kneeling at her feet, squeezing his big body into the space between the bed and the chair.

His damp white shirt proudly displayed the hard musculature of his back, tapering down to a narrow waist. The man was too beautiful for words.

When he gripped her calf and tugged one stubborn shoe off, she let her torso pitch forward and pressed her breasts to his back, as if for support. The sensation of those hard, jutting shoulder muscles and bones digging into her soft flesh was indescribable. Nush bit her mouth to bite off the moan that wanted to escape.

He stilled instantly, like a big jaguar scenting prey.

"So this…" she searched for something to say, something to poke his steel trap mind with, "trip is kinda like a honeymoon?"

"No." His fingertips were featherlight on her calf.

"Why not?"

"This isn't a proper honeymoon. More of a work trip. I will take you on a real one as soon as our schedules let up a bit."

"In all the years I've known you, you've never taken a day off," she said, half laughing, half shocked and all too overwhelmed at the matter-of-fact resolve in his words.

"I will do everything to seduce you into giving me this, Princesa," he said, as if he knew exactly what she was thinking. "You should know that."

Golden-brown eyes held hers and Nush trembled. But she refused to let her fears hold her back anymore. For so long, she'd wanted this right to touch him as she pleased. To run her fingers through those thick locks of hair and sift through them.

She did it now, shamelessly, tracing her fingers over the plane of his forehead, tugging at his hair. He bowed his head, as if he was a present to be unwrapped for her pleasure. A half growl, half groan rumbled up through his chest. "I'd protest more if it weren't for the happy pills numbing my chaotic thoughts."

His fingers busied themselves with the other shoe, gentle but firm and all Nush could think of was how those fingers would feel on other places that were desperate for his touch.

"I didn't think you were the type to delude yourself, Nush. The pills don't make you amenable to something you're against. They *maybe* lower your inhibitions."

He straightened on his knees, bringing his face level with hers. One thumb traced her jaw, moving back and forth, his gaze glittering with an intensity that burned through her. "But as set on this as I am, I will give you time to get used to it."

"What does that mean? Are you going to cockblock me again?"

The corner of his mouth lifted up in a parody of a smile as the pad of his wicked thumb danced at the edges of her lip but never really landed. "How did I not know that you had such a dirty mouth?"

"You don't know a lot of things about me," Nush said, trying to act coy and failing miserably. It came out husky and needy and...hoarse.

"You're right. I'm looking forward to being enlightened." Pushing up to stand, he drew her to her feet. "Now, let's get these wet things off you."

"Are you going to make us wait then?" Nush asked, arresting his hands that were busy with the waistband of her leather skirt.

"Wait for what?" he asked, looking just as distracted as she felt.

His fingers had located the side zipper on the skirt before Nush realized he was waiting for a reply.

It was impossible to string words and thoughts together when his hands were all over her. The leather skirt was gently but firmly being nudged off the thick curve of her hips. "Make me wait before we have sex?" she said, uncaring how petulant she sounded. "I guess it's not such a hard-ship for you to wait. You probably even think of it like a task to check off but—"

Suddenly, his fingers were on the parts of her ass that were exposed by the bodysuit and her lacy white panties and she was pressed up against him so tight that a hard, heated length pressed up against her belly. She gripped his bulging bicep as she trembled as the shape and weight of his erection pressed into her soft belly.

For a long, tormenting minute, he just held her like that with his fingers roving and caressing and kneading the plentiful curves of her ass. Up and down they went, tracing the creases, delving nearer but not close enough to the place between her legs that was clenching and releasing and dampening for his touch.

Nush opened her mouth to suck in a breath and tasted his skin. Salt and heat and sweat added to the combustible pleasure waiting to detonate inside. She desperately wanted to move, to seek the friction she needed, but the damned man had her locked up against him.

Caio's mouth stilled against her temple as he held her in place with one hand on her hip. "Still think it's a task on a to-do list, Princesa? I'm thirty-seven years old and yet, every single time I'm near you, I'm in this state, Nush. Ever since you demolished every bit of decency I ever possessed."

Closing her eyes, she breathed in the warm, dark scent of him, let her other senses feast on his need for her. It was a thrumming melody in her blood. At least in this, there was nothing but brutal honesty between them. And still, she needed more. Wanted more. Demanded more.

"Tell me something you want to do to me."

She felt the tension in his body ratchet up. "You like it if I talk as dirty as you do?"

"Yes. And you owe me this, Caio."

A rough bark of a sound that was a cross between a groan and a protest enveloped her "God, you're an insatiable little thing, aren't you?" One finger made a detour down her ass cheek, and stilled. "But I don't owe you anything. Not when you think this is all a filthy transaction, Princesa."

The blasted man and his mind games. "Fine. Think of it as a wedding present."

"So it is a wedding when you can use it to get something you want?"

"Yes. I learned negotiation from the best."

He laughed then. And it was a sound different from anything Nush had ever heard before. Desire and want and...joy twined through it, tugging her closer. "I want to lick your nipples, *querida*. Roll them against my tongue and suck them into my mouth. It was all I could think of when you sat across from me after the ceremony today. All pretty and placid and poised, all that fire and passion packed away where only I could reach it. Unraveled only for my pleasure. I wanted to throw everyone out and rip that dress off and take you on the desk."

Just as suddenly, as if he'd revealed too much, he released her.

Eyes wide and breath choppy, she stared at the tight set of his features. He didn't betray by breath or look that he was sporting an erection that made her tingly all over, his control a thing to watch, to marvel at. And Nush wondered what it would take to undo it. To make him as confused and volatile and unraveled as she felt. Not only at a physical level but deeper. Or if that was even possible.

"That thing is going to be tricky," he said in a matter-of-fact voice, pointing to her bodysuit top. "Where does it come off?"

Sticking her fingers between her thighs, Nush undid the press button. The little contact of her fingers where she was desperate to be touched, while he watched, was a trip on its own.

The lower edges of the bodysuit rolled up, the stretchy material released.

His gaze stayed at the juncture of her thighs. With a hard swallow, Nush followed it. She liked his gaze on her—mesmerized, caught, still. The lacy fabric of her panties barely hid anything from him. Thank God she'd let Yana talk her into the spa day. She hated the idea of going completely bald down there but she was all trimmed and tidied.

The sight of his hard swallow made liquid desire thrum through her.

"Let's keep going, shall we?" he said a minute later and she definitely heard the crack in his voice then.

His control was there but it was also paper-thin. She smiled like a clown.

"What are you smiling at?" Caio asked, fingers busy rolling up the fabric of the bodysuit, baring more and more of her.

Nush shrugged and released the tension in her stiff arms. Let him move her until one arm was free of the bodysuit. She stood with her side pressed into his middle as he pulled the top off her head. Now it was just a matter of getting her injured arm free.

"Do you think you can manage if I remove the sling for just a few minutes?"

"The sling is mainly so that I don't forget about my wrist and jostle it."

"Here goes." With slow, light movements, he removed the Velcro from around her neck, all the while cradling her wrist with one hand. "Is that okay?" he asked, releasing her left wrist very gently.

Nush shook her head.

His thick brows drew into a frown, as if outraged by the fact that her body didn't listen to his dictates. "What do you need, Princesa?"

"A kiss would make me feel a lot better."

His nostrils flared, a wicked light dawning in his tawny gold eyes. "Let me get these wet things off you, Princesa, and you can have whatever you want."

"I want it now," she demanded sulkily, tipping her chin up. "I got married, lost a fortune in stock to my greedy fake husband, then got sent out while he hung out with his ex for hours on end behind closed doors with everyone giving me pitying looks, then I got hurt and then I got wet and then I got kidnapped and it's really not a stretch to want some kind of compensation for all the—"

His mouth swallowed her complaint.

Fingers gripped her head while he...*devoured* her. This kiss was rough, demanding, hard. Full of teeth and nips. His long fingers tangled in her hair, gripping it, twisting it, and Nush moaned. If he'd been gentle with her, she might have fallen apart. But he wasn't. He let her feel his hunger, his threadbare control, his raw need and that was the best present he could've ever given her.

Nush pressed into him, loving the scent and feel of him, craving more and more. Every inch of her throbbed, every inch of her needed. He tasted and smelled like all the decadent things in the world, of long, cozy winter nights, and bright sunny afternoons and everything in between.

Dragging his mouth away from hers, he trailed soft kisses down her jaw and at her neck and before she knew it, he was moving away. Still reeling from the dizzying sensation, she looked down to find him kneeling at her feet. Dampness made her sex ache and she couldn't help but press her thighs together.

"What…what are you doing?"

"Giving you a kiss to make up for all the hardship you had to endure today."

"But I meant…" Cheeks reddening, Nush watched helplessly as his big palms cupped her hips, steadying her. She wanted his mouth there but she also…

"This is the kiss I want to give. The taste I want from my new bride."

Devilish man and his damned games!

"If you're not ready for it, if you're too…tired for it," he said, his voice honey smooth, "I'll put you to bed, *querida*."

The wicked twinkle in his eyes tore through her inhibitions. How dare he insinuate that she wasn't ready for this? For him?

"No, I want it."

"Say it. Beg me for it."

"Caio, will you please go down on me?"

He gave her a smile that was so full of heat and promise that Nush swayed. "Hold on," he said, pulling her other hand to his head.

"I'm fine."

"You won't be when I get started and I don't want you to get hurt more."

She relented and clutched his thick hair.

Hands on her knees, he made her spread her thighs a little more and then he was nosing through her folds, the lace of her panties no barrier.

"You're so pretty all over, Anushka."

And then her panties were ripped off and then he separated her folds and then he was licking her…there.

The differences hit her first.

She was only used to her fingers and even then, she'd always needed lots of help but Caio's tongue… Jesus, he was thorough. He licked her up and around and then stabbed her opening with the tip of his tongue.

Nush thought she might pass out before she came.

"Is that good?"

"Please don't stop."

He chuckled and Nush wasn't beyond begging.

Seeing his dark head between her thighs added its own fuel to the fire he lit with soft, tentative licks. Nush was melting, coming undone, turned inside out. He wasn't applying some practiced technique. He wasn't using whatever experience he had.

He was learning her—every clench of her abdomen, every moan and rasp that escaped her, every shiver that went through her thighs—and he kept up a running narrative, asking her to tell him what felt better, where she wanted more, how fast or slow she wanted it, and God, it was a whole experience.

And then he applied all of that knowledge and Nush thought she'd drown but he didn't and then he was sucking at her clit and she was panting and then he was working his broad finger into her, and the wicked light in his eyes when he met hers for a fraction of a second, the shuddering inhale he took as if he needed the scent of her in his lungs and then more sucking of her tender flesh and she splintered apart. Hard. Shaking. Sobbing.

She screamed his name and even the momentary mortification that everyone on the flight could hear her didn't stop her.

Caio stayed on his knees, steadying her and holding her, kissing her and whispering praise, as if she'd done the work, until the last flutter died down.

Nush ran her fingers through his hair, a fizzy smile on her lips. "I'll make you one promise."

"And what's that, Princesa?"

"I'm willing to give this a temporary try if that's on the menu regularly."

With a growl of laughter, Caio shot to his feet and kissed her and she could taste herself on him and she wondered if it could truly be like this— full of laughter and pleasure.

It wouldn't be, the sensible part of her replied. It was just pheromones talking.

But if it was all she could get out of this for now—his kisses and his caresses and this intimacy with him—then Nush would take it. And cherish it when it was over. When things fell apart and when Caio realized he didn't need this arrangement of theirs anymore.

CHAPTER NINE

NUSH HAD NEVER believed in love at first sight. That was until she'd seen the house on the island that Caio had personally overseen the restoration of in the last few months by his own admission.

Everything that had stood before had been razed to the ground, he'd told her, because the very foundation of it had been rotting from the inside. And what he'd had built in its place had stolen a piece of her heart.

Three floors of honey-colored, hand-grained hardwood floors, huge open spaces with exposed beams and sloping ceilings and loads of light, three-hundred-and-sixty-degree glass walls with views of the ocean and a few splashes of color in the form of local art, the house was an architectural marvel. An infinity pool, a second-level deck with a hot tub, and on the beautiful grounds, an orange grove, there was so much to explore. White walls and white furniture and simple but elegant touches made the house warm and welcoming, even in its austerity. Like Caio himself.

We can live here part of the year if you like it, he'd said, eyes dancing with pleasure when she'd gushed over the sloping roof and the orange bougainvillea creeping up and covering all of one side of the house. *We need only return to your grandparents' house when Mira or Yana are visiting*, he'd added.

Nush had simply smiled, excited to explore rooms upon rooms but loathe to give her assent to his determined plans for their future. Not even to please him in the moment could she give in.

Though it was far from easy to resist.

He kept dangling such scenarios in front of her, drugging kisses laced with whispered demands that she take that final step with him— pretty much her fantasy and dream future rolled up into alluringly aching promises, and she tried her best to not react, to not reach for everything he offered. To retain some sense of self-preservation.

The first couple of days, she'd been sleeping and eating as her wrist had been hurting a lot more than she'd expected. Then she explored the house, one expansive enough to raise the big, boisterous family she'd always dreamed of having. Which led her to wonder if Caio felt the same.

How could he when he was tight-lipped about his own family, when in the fifteen years she'd known him, he'd never even mentioned them except for his father? Even then it had been to draw her out. As many times as she'd probed about the acquisition, he'd batted away her curiosity by distracting her.

She had let it go. For now. Especially since she'd barely seen him in the week since they'd arrived. He'd even apologized for leaving her alone for so many days.

Having fended for herself during her childhood and early adolescence, the quiet solitude didn't bother her one bit. She'd simply got back to work on the pending software model. The rest of the time she explored the grounds and the beach and kept in touch with her sisters.

She called Mira, who was in Athens, daily and was glad to hear that she and Aristos were giving their marriage a second chance. Which had been a love match.

At least that was what she and Yana had assumed when their reserved, practical sister had turned up married after one weekend in Vegas to a man she'd barely known.

Yana was harder to pin down as she traveled for shoots all over the world. Still, she texted whenever she could, sometimes in twenty to thirty strings of one-sided conversation, and Nush loved seeing her sister's naughtiness come through.

So Nush would've been content. Except for Caio, who seemed determined to control how much he was prepared to open up to her. Though to be fair, he was gone before she woke up and when he returned, she was knocked out by the pills.

On the couple of occasions that she'd been awake when he'd crawled into bed, freshly showered and in silk boxers she'd barely got a peek at, he'd peppered her with questions about the day, about design elements for the model she was currently working through on paper, about Mira and Yana and any number of things. All about her, while venturing nothing about his day or himself.

And Nush was beginning to see how easily he distracted her every time she asked after his family or his past or even the acquisition that had been so important to him.

Soon, Princesa. Once I have everything in place, was all he would say.

Another time his abrupt taunt had been, *When you give me your commitment, when you promise me you're with me for the long term, Anushka, you'll know all the dirty details of my past.*

Even in her half-asleep state, she'd wondered at what he didn't want to share with her.

Worse, only now, in broad daylight, did she realize that he was both surprised and displeased that she was holding out on him, could she see how he used her artless desire for him as a tool to distract her.

Just last night, she'd been awake enough for once to see the bleakness in his eyes, the hard twist of his mouth when she'd walked into the bathroom and found him staring at his reflection in the mirror.

Her heart had ached for the pain stamped all over him. And yet when she'd hugged him from behind and begged him to tell her what was eating at him, all he'd said was that he needed her. And she'd felt him channeling all of that pain into his caresses as he'd carried her back to their bed.

He'd kissed her and teased her with those clever fingers, his hard chest pressed against her back and her legs raised and open in an indecent but utterly erotic position that had made her sex clench greedily.

It had been the most gloriously slow climb to the peak, as he touched her slowly at first, then fast, then penetrated her with one, two and then three fingers, introducing her to a sweet, painful burn that made the pleasure he doled out in controlled measures all the more lush and welcoming. Like he was in every other walk of life, the man was extraordinarily thorough with her body, and the cues she gave, driven by some feral need that he'd learn every inch of her body and what turned her on, what made her sigh and groan and scream, that had driven him to drag out her orgasm for so long that when it had hit her finally, it had left her fractured and sobbing at the intensity of it.

Caio had held her with a tender reverence that had calmed her, coaxed her down from the volatile energy of her release, pressed soft kisses to her damp brow all the while whispering to her that her willingness and vulnerability were a gift he'd relish unwrapping again and again.

But even in the part Vicodin and part orgasm-fueled molasses that had been her mind, she'd known that he hadn't let her touch him.

As if whatever had chased him during the day needed to be cleansed by splintering her apart and putting her back together all over again.

If she hadn't felt him, thick and hard against her behind, she'd have thought he wasn't affected at all. But he'd been. There had been a desperate intensity to his caresses but he asked nothing of her.

Nush might have let it go until she'd seen the email that had popped up in her inbox by accident. Until she called Peter Sr. and inquired after the acquisition Caio was working on and learned that Thaata had been expressly against the very thing. Which explained why he hadn't left the stock to Caio.

Caio hadn't lied to her and yet he'd hidden something big from her.

Every question of hers about the acquisition had been unanswered. Worse, he'd distracted her, used her own desire against her.

Even now, as she walked back into the house after an early evening stroll through the orange grove and donned a swimsuit for a soak in the hot tub, she decided things would have to change.

Caio walked into the deck that provided a spectacular view of the sunset over the dark waves of the ocean providing a symphony. With the orange horizon behind her kissing the silky golden brown of her bare shoulders, and the flimsy triangles of her bikini top drawing his attention to the swells of her breasts, she was a sight he wondered if he could ever get used to. Jets of water bubbled around her, kissing all that bare skin and it was all he wanted to do.

The first few days, it had been extremely disconcerting to find Nush in his bed, tangled up in the sheets, arms and legs thrown akimbo, thick wavy locks of her hair spread over his pillow. Smiling in the dark, he'd collected various arms and legs and bed covers and slowly tucked her to his side, making sure she didn't jostle her wrist.

He didn't remember the last time he'd had a woman sleeping in his bed. Probably never. Even when he and Sophia had been together, it had been all hush-hush, a dirty secret she hadn't wanted to reveal to anyone. Being led by his groin and by the idea of thwarting his stepbrother, his nineteen-year-old self had found it intensely satisfying. He'd been a poor, gullible bastard.

It hadn't taken longer than a day for him to get used to Nush there. And worse, every evening he returned wondering if she would still be there. His rational mind knew she didn't know of his activities during the day and yet, with her probing questions about his family, about the acquisition, it wouldn't be long before she'd know what he was up to. Before he couldn't hide the reality of who he was from her anymore.

And the more she resisted giving him her commitment, the more he resisted giving her the truth, and the more he didn't want to let her go.

Because for all the years and strategies he'd spent to corner his stepfather like a hunted animal, Caio hadn't calculated how he'd feel when he'd arrived there. Of how empty and dissatisfied and purposeless it would all seem. How his half brother Javier's face as Caio refused to see him again would torment him.

Cristo, it should've been a celebratory moment. He should've felt free. Instead all he felt was…this feeling of betrayal.

Neither did it escape his notice that he was using Nush as a balm to cover that emptiness, that she deserved more, but he couldn't bring himself to care anymore.

Finishing his drink, he started unbuttoning his shirt when she became aware of his presence.

A fine tremor went through her shoulders as she turned to look at him, and wiped at the steam on her face. Her gaze landed on his bared throat and skidded away. "You're back. Before the middle of the night."

While the idea of aggravating her to the point where her explosive temper let him tease out that passion of hers was incredibly tempting, he didn't want to manipulate her. Not today, when he needed something real and raw like only Nush could give him, to bring him back to balance. To rid the aftertaste of what he'd done. "Shall I join you?" he asked, the wariness in her eyes playing havoc with his need.

"No." The weight of the single word had his fingers stilling on the buttons. "I'm ready to get out and if you want to take a shower, we can have dinner together after."

"You still haven't eaten?" he said, checking his watch, which said a quarter to eight.

"Nope," she said popping the *p*, which confirmed she was indeed mad about something. "And really, Caio, just because my wrist is broken doesn't mean I don't know how to look after myself. I've done it for ages."

He raised his palms in surrender.

Her mouth, in turn, pursed tight in a way that was just unnatural for her. Fighting the urge to tease it open with his fingers and then something else—God, she was nowhere near ready for that particular fantasy of his—he cleared his throat. "Did Maria leave anything in the refrigerator?"

"No offense but I don't know how you can eat her cooking," she said, pulling up to her knees, giving him a better view of the bikini top hugging her breasts.

His hands itched to cup their delicious weight before bringing them to his lips. Her nipples tightened to stiff points, making his mouth water for a taste.

"Her food is bland and boring. Is vegetarian lasagna okay? Or does not eating red meat for an evening offend your delicate masculine sensibilities?" she asked with a sniff that made him laugh until tears burned his eyes.

She stared at him, rapt. "You're gorgeous when you…laugh. When you just let yourself be…real."

"As opposed to what, Anushka?"

"As opposed to employing strategies and distractions with me, as opposed to treating this thing between us like some kind of deal you're finessing," she finished in a soft voice that only underlined her anger.

"Let me help you out of there and we—"

She scooted away in the hot tub when he reached out to help her. The edge of his own temper flared, like a little boy denied his favorite toy. He wasn't unaware of how…invested he was getting in this, in her, but it only a warning at the edge of his consciousness. Nothing but a vague, discordant threat drowned out by his current obsession with pleasing her, making her smile, making her explode with his fingers and mouth.

Whatever she saw in his gaze, she offered a mollifying "I can manage it. Go ahead and shower."

"Is there a problem if I want to help my injured wife out of a slippery hot tub?" he asked, undoing and pushing the cuffs of his shirt back.

Her gaze dipped to his bare chest and lingered. Before sweeping down onto his abdomen and then she licked her lower lip. Heat poured through him like thick honey at the stark desire etched onto her features. "Nush?" he said, incapable of teasing her. It felt like his control was hanging on by its last, frayed thread.

She looked up and blushed fiercely. "We've barely talked in the last week and I'd prefer it if we—"

"Is that why you're angry? Because I was gone so much?"

"Of course not," she said, genuinely confused that he'd think so. "You told me you'd be busy and contrary to your preconceptions, I handle solitude better than most. But for tonight, I have some ground rules."

"And what are those?"

"For starters, you're not allowed to touch me."

His curse could have been heard at the beach. His own anger flared to match hers. "That's not a rule. More like personal pettiness that's not worthy of you." Suddenly, he'd turned into the man-child that still remembered the shattering pain of his mama abandoning him, casting him out into the world. Choosing his stepfather and his half brothers above him. "And you know what, Princesa? Fine. I don't care. I won't touch you if that's what you want." Somehow, he arrested the hurtful words that wanted to clamor out of him.

But the damned minx didn't back down one

bit. "Okay then. If it's that much of a deal breaker for you to let me have some say in this, there's no point in me pretending that I belong here. You already got what you wanted, yeah? So let me go, Caio. Let's call this farce what it is. I want to go home first thing tomorrow morning."

"No," he said, his mouth twisting in a wounded snarl. "Your home is with me."

Her gaze held his—not just defiant but beseeching too. "Choose, Caio, then. Choose me. Right now. Choose me because you want a future with me. Choose me for myself, not for the stock in the company or to save your face or to acquire something else you've been coveting for years. Choose me because you can't let me go."

"Jesus, Anushka," he said, staring at her. Cristo, the woman had a multitude of weapons against him and yet, for once he didn't mind losing. Even as she dictated terms to him, he found himself wanting to kiss that mouth, to taste that fierceness. "When did you turn so bloodthirsty?"

"You're not the only one who can be determined and aware of their power in this relationship."

"For once, I've no idea what you're thinking." He rubbed a hand over his forehead. "Why am I not allowed to touch you?"

Her smile was full of a wicked triumph he wanted to taste despite his own fury coursing through him. "I want to talk tonight and if you touch me, we'll go off-script."

His mouth twitched, his anger leaving as fast as it came. "How's that?"

"Hmm? You'll touch me to lift me out and then I'll want to kiss you and you'll oblige and I'll sweetly beg for an orgasm and you'll make me work for it, prolonging every caress and kiss and by the time I climax, I'll be so exhausted that I'll want to crawl into bed and you'll pat me and tuck me in as if I've been a good little girl and out the window go all my intentions…" She let out a long breath, a line appearing between her brows.

"That you can't keep your hands and mouth off me is the biggest turn-on I've ever known. Don't take that away from me, Princesa."

"It is when you use my desire for you like a weapon against me," she said, her voice thick and full of unshed tears. "That has to stop. Now."

Twin flames danced in her big eyes and he found himself floundering in them. How had he not realized that the quiet, shy teenager he'd teased had turned into a magnificent woman who could hold her own against him? How could he tell her that it was only with her that he felt even this much?

"You have to stop treating me as if I'm some imbecile teenager with a crush on you."

"You know me more than I have ever let anyone else know me, Princesa."

"I'm not in a competition with others in your life, Caio. Neither am I some kind of complimentary prize you're letting yourself have. Because if that's how you see me, then..." she swallowed and looked away, "then this is over. Now."

Caio flinched at how close to the truth she'd got. "Threatening me, Princesa?"

"No. Setting some ground rules." An ache he hated seeing glowed in her eyes. "I should've known that that's the only way to get anywhere with you."

"That's unfair."

"As unfair as hiding that you went against Thaata's express wishes when you used your executive power to push through that acquisition? Or the way you distract me every time I get close to the truth?"

"I thought your loyalty was to me, Nush."

If he thought the bitterness in his voice would shake her, he was wrong. "It is to you, Caio. I don't care why you did it or even that you went against Thaata, to be honest. But you...you don't respect me enough to let me—"

The clamor in his chest quieted as fast as it had begun. Ignoring her squeals of protest, Caio locked his hands at her back and lifted her out and when she could kneel on the edge of the tub, he kept her there. Miles of bare, wet skin greeted his hands and he stroked and petted every inch shamelessly. "You're wrong if you think I see you as any less than the magnificent woman you are, Nush. Why the hell do you think I've let it come this far? Why do you think I jumped on the chance to make you mine forever?"

Her eyes widened in her face, her mouth trembled. "You're not lying."

"No. I choose you, Nush. Never believe anything else. And if it's truth you want, then you'll have it. In all its ugly glory."

She stared at him, her mouth glistening, her eyes full of those unshed tears again. "I'm getting you all wet," she whispered hoarsely, her breasts crushed against his chest.

"I don't care," he said, and then he kissed her.

It was a rough claiming. A branding, even he couldn't deny it. An arrogant declaration that she was his to kiss, to rumple up, to tease and taunt as he pleased.

He poured every ounce of heat that had been simmering through him all day into the kiss. Fingers twisting in her hair, he laved at that lower lip until she opened up with a groan. He scored his teeth over her neck and licked a trail over the marks. When her spine arched and she pushed into his touch he took her nipple, covered by the flimsy fabric of her top, into his mouth and sucked at it. When she sobbed, he dragged the cup down and laved the aching bud with reverent strokes. When she grabbed his face with shaking hands, he plunged into the warm cavern of her mouth, as if he were a parched man finally reaching home.

And to him, after everything he'd put in motion today, Nush was coming home.

With a growl that made him impossibly hard, she bit his lower lip and that in turn gentled and calmed the ravenous beast inside him.

Drawing his fingertips down the line of her spine gently, he let her claim him in return. The twin swords of her innocence and her sensuality were like a cleansing fire that left him shaking. Her own aggression died down in a few seconds, like his had. Fingers clasped at the nape of his neck, she pressed her face to the hollow at his throat. Even then, her tongue flicked out and licked him there and he let out a guttural growl.

She hid her face again and a wave of tenderness shook him. "Why haven't you slept with me yet then?" The question came out in a soft, cloaked whisper as though it had somehow slipped out before she could intone it better.

"I sleep with you every night, Princesa," he said, keeping his own words free of tease. "In fact, I think it should be one of the primary tenets of our marriage. We always go to bed together, no matter what."

Looking up, she searched his gaze as though to check if he was being facetious. "That's a good rule. But I haven't agreed to calling this a marriage yet."

"Why didn't I know how stubborn you can be?"

"Why didn't I know how manipulative you can be?" she returned on the next breath.

Caio laughed and the sound was full of a relief that filled him. Hope sprung in his chest despite the bitter ground his mother had left behind. Could Nush see him for who he was and still want him?

"On an intellectual level, I know that it's not because you don't want me. But on another level, I know that you're playing a game with me. Holding out on me. I might even call it sexual blackmail because I didn't immediately fall into line with your plans."

He tilted her chin up to face him. "I am surprised by your resistance, yes. But you give me diabolical motives I'm not guilty of. You know I've been too busy to even have dinner with you. And I wanted to give you time to get used to this."

"So no sex until I give in to your permanent partnership deal?"

Smiling, he ran his fingers over her cast. "You've been using that hand too much with work and now cooking. I also…" he cleared his throat, searching for words so that he didn't embarrass her, "know that you haven't done this before, Nush."

"Done what?"

"Had sex."

"Oh." She blushed then, so prettily that he couldn't help grinning. "Of course, you could tell with how busy your fingers have been."

His chest shook with mirth. "I wasn't going to be all over you, demanding my marital rights after realizing that."

She giggled and it was the sweetest sound Caio had ever heard.

"It's not a big deal, Caio. Yes, some of it was that I was hung up on—"

He pressed a hand to her mouth, his heart thudding as if it had been slammed hard against its cage. "You don't have explain anything to me, *querida*. It just…made me put brakes on how fast I was driving this, that's all."

"I like fast, Caio. I love your speed very much. And you should know that if you were going too fast, I'd protest quite loudly." Then she rubbed the tip of her nose against his in a tender gesture that burned him. "You have to stop making accommodations for me, Caio, as if I were not strong enough to handle you. You've got to trust that I know my own mind."

He nodded, wondering what benevolent god had dropped her into his lap. Because he sure as hell didn't deserve her. "It might hurt, Nush. However much I try to make it better."

"Then isn't it better to get the first time out of the way so that we can get to the better times?"

He shook his head and pulled her up. "Wrap your legs around me."

"Why?"

"You're tiring, Princesa. Let's get you into the shower."

That she didn't deny it told him he was right. "How'd you know?"

"The more it bothers you, the more you cradle your wrist to your chest like a shield." He hefted her into his arms and walked through the house, her outraged giggles that they were ruining the hardwood floors by getting everything wet ringing in his ear. Her laughter reverberated through the empty, desolate house as did her breath through him.

And that small part of him he could never quite shut up asked if she'd let him hold her like that if she knew of the destruction he was wreaking, if she knew how close to the truth she'd come when she'd called him manipulative and controlling and arrogant and how he could lose the battle to win a war.

CHAPTER TEN

I CHOOSE YOU, NUSH. The words reverberated through Nush like temple bells, restoring her faith in their relationship at a deep, core level where all her insecurities dwelled like sleeping monsters.

By the time she emerged from the shower, hair still mostly damp because she didn't have enough strength in her one weak bicep to dry her thick hair, Caio had arranged everything outside in the patio off the kitchen.

A soft melody belted out from cleverly hidden speakers, the words in Portuguese. Running a hand over her dress, she reminded herself to ask him to teach her the language. She wanted to be able to converse with him in his mother tongue, which was a long-term project for her brain. But more than that, she wanted to understand all the things he muttered to her when he touched her.

He'd set the plates already served with lasagna she'd made, a salad he seemed to have whipped up, a bottle of wine and glasses. A couple of sleek solar heaters kept the space toasty even as a breeze from the ocean tickled its cold fingers once in a while.

Beautiful, rare black roses sitting in a crystal vase at the center of the small table sent her pulse racing all over her body like a loose electrical wire. That he'd remembered what Yana called her morbid fascination with all things dark and decadent made her dizzy with joy.

His hair, like hers, was still wet from the shower and slicked back. He'd dressed in dark jeans and a gray Henley that seemed to span an endlessly broad chest. The sexy casual attire made the dinner feel even more intimate. Like here was another side of Caio Oliveira revealed just for her and only for her pleasure. And God, what those jeans did to that ass.

Feeling suddenly self-conscious, Nush wished she'd taken the time and patience to dry her hair properly. All she'd done in terms of dressing up had been to pull on a loose, sleeveless pink gown with a deep V at the front and slap a little lip gloss onto her lips. After all the fuss she'd made about dining together, maybe she should have…

"Princesa? Have I missed something?"

"No. I just…" Nush swallowed her silly doubts at the possessive gleam in his eyes when they swept over her, lingering everywhere it fluttered. "It's perfect."

"You're the one that is perfection, Nush."

She bit her lip and smiled, fighting the urge to smooth her hair down. Longing twisted through her for something more. Even though she kept begging her greedy heart to stop its needy clamor. "Thank you."

"Shall we eat then?"

Nodding, she joined him at the table. He'd arranged the chairs closer together, looking out into the ocean, instead of on opposite sides of the table. Her belly swooped at how romantic it looked.

When they'd settled into the chairs, he poured himself a glass of wine and produced sparkling water for her. "I'd like wine too," she said, forking a piece of the flat noodles into her mouth.

"I thought you couldn't mix alcohol with your meds."

"It's one glass, Caio. And I'm not really planning to drive myself anywhere."

Nush took a sip after he poured and made a face. The dry bitterness drew a caustic trail down her throat. "That tastes…awful."

"That's a ten-thousand-dollar bottle, Princesa," Caio said, looking suitably horrified by her comment even as his mouth twitched. "Maybe you need a discerning palate to enjoy it."

She stuck her tongue out at him. "I think my dad took care of our palate when it comes to enjoying alcohol one way or the other. After seeing him in one of his binges, none of us can stomach alcohol in any form."

He stared at her. "Then why did you insist I pour you some?"

"Because you decided I couldn't have any," Nush said, biting her lip.

"Stubborn minx."

"Arrogant, high-handed stud."

His laughter provoked her own and they busied themselves with the cutlery.

"I didn't realize how it must affect you, or Yana or Mira, to see him like that."

Nush shrugged. "Mira's the one who's seen him at his worst, who's terrified that that kind of addiction runs in her veins."

"You?"

She shivered and instantly, Caio placed a jacket over her shoulders. "My fears lie in a different place."

His fork clattered to the plate with a loud clank in the silence. "Where?"

"It's not a big deal. Neither is it something you can immediately fix for me."

His brows tied together in a dark scowl. Breath hitching in her chest, Nush watched him.

The wineglass turned round and round in his

large hand. "But you know that I'd try anyway, don't you? To fix them for you?"

She swallowed, an overwhelming sense of affection surging through her. Turning away, she took a bite of her food, knowing that any of her attempts to hide from him were only half-hearted. She couldn't play games like him, couldn't control her thoughts and feelings around him in some kind of transaction. A sigh left her. "Promise me you won't think me less for it?"

His golden-brown gaze held hers in a solemn promise. "There's nothing in the world you could tell me that would make me think less of you."

"Mama's mental health problems…are hereditary." She touched his wrist when he'd have spoken up. "I know it's not a guarantee that I'll get them, only that there's a probability higher than…yours, for example. My fear is not even that I'll inherit them. But more irrational…"

"Like what?"

"My recurring nightmare is that I'll be left alone in some clinic, forgotten, with no one to visit me, that I'll just fade away under the kindness of strangers."

With a soft curse, Caio gathered her to him, his arms a steel band around her. "It's never going to come to that, Nush. You're never going to be alone like that. Never."

"I loathe the idea of becoming some kind of burden on you."

"Is that how you think of your mother?"

"Of course not," she said, recoiling at the very thought. "I just… I have a hard time, still, believing that this is all real, Caio. That you want to spend your life with me. That it's not a…"

An angry growl escaped from his mouth, making her pull back from the pit of her own insecurities. "What do I do to prove to you that I want this?"

"You don't have to prove anything to me," she said, alarmed by the hard edge of anger and something more in his voice. "Proofs and transactions and contracts…those won't bind us."

"You're being purposely stubborn about this. Turning this into a battle."

"I'm not, Caio, believe me. Choosing the hard way is Yana's style. Not mine. I just…want this, have wanted this for too long, with everything in me, to let it be anything but real. I'm not holding out on you because I don't want this. But because I…want it too much."

Even out of her periphery, she could see the tension around him deflate at her honest confession.

Hard knuckles dragged down her cheek as he said, "Okay, let me ask you something. Would you turn back on me, desert me if you discov-

ered a new facet to me? If you learned that I...
have a real deficiency? Not a mental health
problem like you worry about, which makes no
woman or man less. If I have a weakness that
has been bred into me as a product of cruel circumstance?"

It was her turn to stare at him. There had been
something in his voice as he said that, a certainty
that there was some dark facet of him that he'd
never let her see. Yes, he was ruthless, and ambitious and had an armor that was probably made
of platinum but... And even the question was
more dare. As if he was playing with her concept of loyalty and commitment.

"If it's some kind of test, it's a horrible one,"
she said, reaching for the wine. Wanting to wash
away the taste of fear from her mouth.

"It's not, Princesa."

"Of course I wouldn't desert you."

"Then you also know that I'd never let you be
alone like that, Nush," he said, "no matter what
happened between us."

Nush blinked back tears, his promise taking
the edge off her deepest fear.

Throwing her own rules out the window, she
nuzzled her face into the side of his neck, loving
the scent of him, the rough texture of his skin
even though he'd just shaved. When she pressed
a soft kiss under his ear, his fingers on her arm

tightened. With a smile, she catalogued his re-action away.

Her erratic heartbeat settled back into a slow rhythm as she pulled back into her seat.

For a while, they ate in silence, his vow taking on a new depth and breadth between them, mor-phing into another concrete layer in the founda-tion of their relationship. Not that everything had been addressed, she knew that.

But it was progress and she reveled in the quiet joy of sharing the moment with him.

"How did I not know that you're such phe-nomenal cook?" he asked, patting his flat ab-domen.

Pleasure filled her like colorful bubbles in a jar at the sight of his empty plate. "I'm full of untold delights like that."

"No arguments there." He kissed her knuck-les. "You're like a present I'll unwrap forever, Princesa."

Heat crested her cheeks and Nush cleared her throat. "If you keep saying things like that, I'll melt into goo, and you'll have to scrape me off this lovely patio."

Elbow on the table, he leaned toward her and licked her upper lip. "How's it that you exchange filthy talk like a pro but blush fiercely at simple compliments?"

She bunched the neck of his sweatshirt in

her fingers and licked him back, inviting him to do more.

No, she didn't have to wait for him to do anything. He was hers for taking, for mussing up, for reveling in, to do as she pleased. For now, at least.

Bolstered by the thought, she took his mouth in a hungry kiss, pouring every ounce of her need into it.

She moaned when he nipped her lower lip and his tongue swooped into her mouth. The kiss intensified yet again, as if there was nothing but heated embers between them to be stoked into life at the barest contact. Flaring hotter and higher with each day that passed, each layer of vulnerability that was ripped off.

His mouth came back for her—nipping, licking, demanding. Demanding so much that Nush felt like she was nothing but a mass of sensations. God, the man kissed like a hungry beast. As if only devouring her would do. As if she was the only thing in the entire universe. And still, this kiss was different from the other ones. As if there were a million different flavors to be yet discovered between them.

He growled when she pulled away to whisper, "God, Caio. We could be together for seventy years and I'd think I'll want you with this same desperate need."

"Give me your vow, Nush. Give me what I want."

Burying her face in his chest, she whispered, "I'm yours, Caio. And not just because those papers say so."

He held her tightly then, with more affection than passion, she thought. Just like their kisses, this embrace was different from all others.

"How did you learn about the acquisition?" He asked then, and Nush felt the instant change in the tenor around them. His arms around her stiffened. And his embrace went from warm Brazilian coast to Arctic frost in one second. He didn't push her away as much as he slowly untangled them and turned to face the spectacular view. Was that all it took? Her word that she was in?

"The paperwork… I got cc'd on your email by accident."

Nush watched him guzzle down his wine in the periphery of her vision. She turned in her chair, playing with the edges of her napkin. "I looked it up and noticed that it was your father's company that you mentioned. The small start-up he began at the same time as Thaata did with OneTech. Then I called Peter Sr. and he was all too happy to enlighten me that Thaata was against the buyout too."

For a long time, he said nothing. Nerves stretched tight, Nush simply waited.

"He was," he said, rubbing a hand over his face. The wet slosh of the wine as he refilled his glass felt like a boom around then. "Enough to block me from beyond the grave."

"I thought you needed majority because you wanted to reign as king over those vultures on the board. But you needed the executive power to push through the purchase for a…problem-riddled company."

A dark smile flashed at her. "I like being a king who lords it over them too."

"Why didn't you just tell me it was once your father's company, Caio? I don't care if Thaata thought it was a lost cause."

"You'd have taken my side even if it were a complete loss," he said as a statement, a little warmth coming back to his eyes.

"Yes. Do you know how happy I feel that our partnership has enabled you to buy your father's company back?"

"Don't be so eager to celebrate, Nush," he said, with a sneer that didn't seem to be directed at her. "It's not the happy ending you always want."

The unease in her gut solidified. But Nush refused to let him scare her off the topic. Push her off a subject that had shaped the man she'd married. "Tell me about the company. Please."

He tapped her lips with his fingers. "What a tantalizing puzzle you are, *minha esposa*."

"I don't know what you mean," she said, cheeks heating up.

He leaned down, and took her mouth in a rough, animalistic kiss. It was full of dominance and ego, full of technique and skill employed to leave her panting. To assert his mastery over her senses. Knowing that, she still quivered, a telling dampness at her sex. "Is *handling* me another one of your secret powers, Nush?"

"All I want is to know about the man who shaped you. About your family. About…"

"Do you really need to know, Princesa? Or are you using my reticence as a weapon against me to deny me what I want?"

"You know the answer to the question, Caio. I told you a real marriage is sacred to me. It means being real in the present. But it also means building a future, a future that encompasses so many things that we haven't even touched."

He rubbed the pad of a finger over her lower lip, setting her on fire. "Like what, *querida*?"

"Like kids, Caio. I want a big, boisterous family. I want my kids to be surrounded and loved by family. I want family vacations, school recitals, story times. I want my kids to know that they're loved by their parents, unconditionally. I want them to have everything I didn't as a kid."

His gaze gleamed with emotion as he placed a tender kiss to her lips that made her emotional all over again. "That sounds like…a future I want to be a part of too, Nush."

Nush exhaled roughly. "Right now, you're no more than a stranger to me. A stranger who carefully filters out what information he'll let me have. A stranger who demands I give everything without giving me anything back. That's not the beginnings of a healthy relationship. That's just a transaction."

His mouth flattened as if her words were a direct hit. She wondered if she'd gone too far. With a rough groan, Caio rubbed his hand down his face. "What do you want to know, Nush?"

"Tell me what this acquisition means to you. This company…"

"My father poured his blood and sweat into it. At the height of his career, it was one of the most successful companies in Sao Paulo. And not just by its workforce or market worth either. It prized financial ethics and family values and had a community with shared values at its core. Papa was its beating heart."

The pride and ache in his voice filled her throat with sudden tears. She took his fingers in hers, wanting to provide him with an anchor in the moment. Wanting to ground him here in the present even as he went away to visit some painful place in the past.

He didn't return her clasp like he usually did, nor did the tension in him abate. But Nush held on. "He sounds like an amazing man. I'd have loved to meet him."

He met her eyes then and she saw that he knew that she meant it with all her heart.

"He'd have loved to meet you too, Anushka." He frowned, studying her as if she was an interesting equation he hadn't seen clearly until that precise moment. "In fact, you're both a lot alike."

"How so?"

"Integrity. Generosity. A seemingly infinite well of quiet strength beneath it all." He rattled them off in a matter-of-fact tone. As if he had to distance himself from Nush too as he'd clearly distanced himself from the memories of the man he'd adored. "A distinct lack of self-preservation or cunning required to survive in this cutthroat world."

"Hey," she said, swatting his arm in mock outrage.

"Just speaking the truth, *querida*." And just like that, she understood the deeper significance of his protectiveness of her.

A long exhale made her chest rise and fall. "What happened to him?"

"He died of heart disease when I was thirteen."

"Oh." She didn't utter any trite comforting words. It was clear that it had devastated him as a child. That it continued to wreck him even now. "Is that when the company fell apart?"

"No. It fell apart, year by year, one underhanded contract after another, one corrupt scheme after the other, once his partner took over. When he realized he didn't have long left, Papa signed over the power of attorney to his partner Carlos. My mother..." such stark anguish crossed his features that it froze Nush in acrid fear, "was a simple soul. She never cared about business or politics or wealth. Papa's partner took advantage of her grief, of her loneliness, of her ignorance, married her within a year of Papa passing. Then he proceeded to drive a wedge between her and me, until she asked me to give up my right to the company. By the time I left to live with Rao, she and I...had become strangers to each other."

The carefully dispassionate way he spoke of his mother...only made the truth that much clearer to Nush. It hid a well of unhealed, festering wounds made of nothing but hurt and pain.

She wanted to throw her arms around him then, to simply hold him. But there was a forbidding quality to him, a brittleness that threatened to shatter everything that was new and fragile between them if she so much as touched him.

"When did she die?"

"Two years after I left. I begged her to join

me." Such pure bitterness spewed from his words that Nush wouldn't have been shocked to see them land like acid drops on the air. "But she kept saying her sons needed her."

"Her *sons*?" She wasn't able to keep her shock out of it.

"She has two sons with him. Twins. Jorge and Javier."

Shock turned her words into a whisper. "Your brothers, you mean?"

Another shrug.

Her chest was so tight that she had to force herself to breathe. "You never saw her again?"

He shook his head and upended another glass of wine down his throat.

"I'm so sorry, Caio. I can't imagine…not being able to say goodbye."

"It is what it is, Princesa. Her priorities were different from mine."

Nush wanted to argue, to say she didn't agree with that. She wanted to delve but was it for anything other than to satisfy her curiosity? Was it for any reason other than to poke her finger into an unhealed wound and make it spill forth more poison? But if he didn't talk about this with her, if that hurt wasn't purged…

He's shared this much, Nush. Give it time. That voice distinctly sounded like Thaata and Nush pushed away the more intrusive questions.

"But you've bought the company now," she said, infusing a lightness she didn't feel into her words. "You can build it up bigger and better than before. Bring back all those principles your father valued. Make it a monument to his big heart and values."

Caio stared at her as if she'd suddenly grown two horns, his sensuous mouth twisting into a distasteful slant. "No."

"What do you mean no?" she said, any semblance of remaining the steady, sensible one in this difficult conversation shattering at the resolute will of that single word.

"There's nothing of my father or his legacy left in that company, Nush."

Nush got to her feet, startled by the vehemence of his words. "You bought it to destroy it?" Clarity came like a veil being lifted permanently. "You set your stepfather up to fall, to lose everything, didn't you?"

"Carlos already destroyed everything good about it, Princesa." By the way he spat that name, Nush knew it was his stepfather. "Lured by the idea of more and more profits, he made one bad deal after the other when he had no resources to deliver. His son Enzo embezzled the pension funds of the employees. Carlos is in crippling debt, all the livelihoods under his care ruined, and he was still looking for a payout. All that's left to do is to pull out its very rotten foundation and grind it to nothing, to reduce the rubble to ashes."

Emotions thrashing in her chest, Nush stared at him. She'd always known there was a well of anger and pain under Caio's smooth facade. Had realized, even as a teenager, that something dark fueled his every move. But to know it as vague speculation and to see it were different. To stand in its direct path was terrifying at a soul-deep level. "And you've been planning this for how long?"

"More than a decade."

"That's…horrible." Agitation pushed her words out. This was why her grandfather had been against Caio going ahead with this. Because if he did this, he was permanently shutting down any connection left to his past. With the bad, he was burning down the good too. "To work toward that kind of destruction for years… you'd have to be…empty of all good things."

"Are you already regretting your promises, Nush?" he said, taking in her defensive posture with her arms around her waist. The distance she'd imposed between them.

She pressed a hand to her forehead, refusing to let him make this about her. "I'm just sad that all of his good name, everything your father stood for, it has to come to dust and ashes like this. That everything you…" She plunged her fingers into his hair, feeling as if her own heart suddenly had a crack in it. "This can't be it, Caio. Tell me the truth. Tell me that's what has been hounding you for the past week. Tell me it feels like a defeat."

He pushed away from her touch. "I have everything I've ever wanted—OneTech, you, this house, the whole bloody island—while Carlos will be left with nothing."

Nush didn't point out that his reassurance sounded painfully hollow and empty. "You've clearly thought this through," she said, forcing a semblance of acceptance into her words. Into her heart. For now, at least. This wasn't a wound that would heal immediately, or pain that would wash away from one conversation with her, however much she wanted that for him.

"Don't waste your bleeding heart on this, Nush."

And that felt like a premonition more than a warning.

Nush took her another step back, knowing that both of them needed space to process this. That the threads binding them were still too fragile to bear the heavy weight of her dissent right now, as much as she wanted to scream it at him.

"I'm going to bed."

He didn't look at her then and it felt like this was a defeat too. Like the bridge they were building to each other was already wobbling. "Don't forget your pills, Princesa."

Nush walked away. But she stopped when she reached the massive living room because she couldn't bear to leave him like that. As if he were all alone in the world, even if he didn't say it.

And where it mattered, in the vulnerable places that lived in all of them, that some of them covered up better than others by hiding and shying away in the margins of life, drenched in fear of loss, that some of them replaced with ambition and success and material possessions they didn't even want, Nush knew Caio was less for the loss of his family. Less for not knowing his brothers. Less for shutting down parts of himself. Less than the great man his father had been.

Which meant he had less of himself to give this thing between them, to give her, whereas she'd already given more than she could afford, all that she had.

All in, as always, Nushie-kins? she could almost hear Yana say in her admonishing voice. *Tsk-tsk...learn how to play the game.*

But it wasn't over. Neither Yana nor Caio understood that part. As afraid she was of who Caio was becoming and what was in thefuture for them, she couldn't simply abandon him when he needed her. It wasn't in her.

Only what if he didn't even admit that he

needed her? What if he pushed her away like he'd done with the memories of his mother or the future he could have had with his half-brothers? What if she didn't agree with him and he decided he'd had enough of her too?

Could she walk away from him tonight knowing how closed off he was? Knowing he was choosing destruction and more pain when he could have something else?

No.

But it couldn't be finished as easily as that. Not when their story was just beginning. Not when he'd stood by her side through all her hard times.

"Caio?"

Her breath came easy when he turned and met her eyes.

"Was that our first big fight?" she said, half laughing, half crying, throwing him a rope and asking him to grab it with both hands.

His head dipped, his forearms braced on his knees, his wineglass dangling precariously between his fingers. "I don't know." Looking up, his gaze pinned her where she stood. Hunger and heat arced into life between them with a snap like an electric whip. "But you got what you wanted, Princesa," he said with a soft growl. "You know now what I'm made of. If you want to break your word, Nush, now's the time. Before I—"

"I think it was a fight," she said, shutting down

his line of thinking. She smiled then, through the tears in her eyes, and the furrow between his brows cleared. "When you're ready to make up, you know where to find me."

His golden eyes gleamed again, that faraway look dissipating instantly. "Yeah?"

"Yeah. I want to make up the fun way. I hear that's the only good thing about fighting as a couple. And Caio?"

"Yes, Princesa?"

"I want to be your wife. Tonight, in every way that matters." Finally, she was beginning to understand him. Was beginning to know the real him—hard, cutting edges and all. And if he wanted her in his life, then he'd have to know her as her too. And that was someone who wouldn't let him make a wrong decision, someone who hated seeing him in pain. "Don't make me wait."

"Is that a threat?" he said, back to playing that wicked game of his.

"Yes," Nush said throwing herself all the way in. "But it's also an entreaty."

She didn't wait to see his reaction but she heard his pithy curse and she wondered that for all the games Yana had played all her life, her sister had never managed to understand the subtle tactic that sometimes to win, one had to surrender completely first.

CHAPTER ELEVEN

THE SOFT BUSS of lips at her cheek instantly awoke Nush from a restless slumber. "Caio?" she whispered, her hands reaching out for him automatically.

His rough, calloused hands took hers, as her eyes got used to the darkness of the bedroom. He'd been standing by the bed on her side, bending over to kiss her. A thread of fear wound through her and words rushed out through a dry mouth. "Are you leaving?"

"No. Of course not. I only meant to check on you, make sure you didn't tangle yourself up in the sheets. You're the most violently active person in sleep."

"Oh," she whispered, feeling a flicker of joy at her chest. In the big scheme of things, it wasn't a big deal that he knew her sleep habits or that he'd wanted to check on her. But to her silly heart, it was a huge thing.

"I didn't mean to disturb you. Go back to sleep, *querida*."

When he'd have pulled away, Nush tightened her grasp of him. "No, wait."

His white smile flashed in the darkness and she breathed out in relief. She saw him thrust his hand through his hair, and sigh. "I demolished the entire bottle of wine, I'm in a sullen mood and sleep is far away for me, Nush. I'll only disturb yours."

Swallowing, Nush pushed up until she was half sitting, supported by her elbow and his tight grip. "I didn't mean to upset you by raking up... Earlier, I mean," she said, wanting to soothe him.

Caio rarely ever let her see him in a dark mood and clearly, she'd breached some invisible boundary she hadn't even known existed.

"You didn't upset me. It's not something that's...ever far from my mind."

Nush swallowed the urge to say that that was by design. His ruthless pursuit of the company, this house even...he'd made the loss of everything a part of himself. He'd turned it into the fuel that drove him. And like a virus, it thrived inside him.

His thumb traced the plump veins on the back of her hand, the touch infinitely gentle. "It's okay if you do upset me."

"I know that," she said, grinning cheekily. "I

just meant that I didn't mean to upset you tonight. Especially not when I want you in a favorable mood."

His grin made her feel as if she'd won the biggest prize in the world. "And why did you want me in a favorable mood?"

"I'm bad at this, Caio," she said, hiding half her face in the pillow. "Fighting with you, I excel at. Throwing dirty talk in your face to rile you up, give me a diploma already. But this...the real thing... I need you to drive this."

His palm covered the other half of her face, encasing it completely. Nush had imagined all kinds of scenarios between them and yet she'd never expected the tenderness with which he constantly touched her. And that made her realize that he did touch her a lot. Outside of sexual context. As if it were as necessary as breath.

Her chest felt like an enlarged balloon, full of wonder and joy and more.

"You're better at it than you think you are."

"Then stay, please." She placed a kiss at the center of his palm, and then licked the spot. His indrawn breath filled the air around them. Egged on by it, Nush dug her teeth into the thick pad of his palm and the tension radiating from him increased a hundredfold. Then she blew on the hurt she'd given him, pressing soft kisses to his wrist.

His thumb traced her lips and then plunged into her mouth. She gave it the same thorough treatment, nipping and biting and licking, sucking on it, until his harsh breathing was a symphony in the room.

"I am a little drunk, Princesa. I might not be—"

"Jesus, Caio, when will you understand that I trust you more than I've ever trusted another person? Even myself at times." Her voice had risen, something electric arcing through her words.

Bringing her hand to his face, Caio buried it in her palm. "That's what makes this so hard. I'm not sure I deserve it."

"I told you. That's not how any of this works. There's no deserving when it comes to..." She swallowed the words that automatically rose to her lips, feeling as if she'd suddenly been plunged into ice-cold water. "Stop making me beg you."

"Turn on the night lamp," he said, command and desire in it making his voice deeper and heavier than she'd ever heard before.

She remained silent, and unmoving, suddenly nervous at the prospect of what she'd wondered for years. It wasn't that she was insecure about her body so much as she wanted to please him. Having tried multiple times with not-quite-unpleasant partners, and then freezing halfway through, she didn't want to face the same mental block again with Caio of all people.

The lamp turned on and she blinked. When she lifted her eyes, Caio was leaning over her, his broad chest tantalizingly bare and within reach. He bent and took her mouth in a gentle, soft kiss that made her heart crawl up into her throat. "I will be as gentle as you need, Princesa."

"Tell me what you like, please," she whispered against the tug of his teeth, her body arching off the bed toward him like a magnet.

"Touch me. Whatever you want to do to me will please me, Nush. That you want me like you do makes me half-hard most of the time."

Nush didn't have to be told again. She ran her hands over his chest in mindless circles, relishing everything about him. Christ, every inch of him was delineated and defined. The hard, defined pecs, the springy hair sprinkled throughout, the rippling definition of his abdomen muscles, the taut musculature of his back and the dark trail of hair lower that disappeared into his jeans…everything about him appealed to her starved senses. Every cell in her arched up to feel and absorb as much of him as possible.

His rough growl at her mouth when she raked her fingernails down his stomach egged her on.

Everything was contrasts—the roughness of his kiss and the softness of his lips, the light bursting behind her eyes and the darkness that surrounded them, the bubbling lightness that spread through her that she was finally, finally, doing this with the man she'd wanted for so long.

Her eyes drew closed even as the kiss morphed from lazy, tender exploration to something else. Something hungry and needy and dirty.

"Let's get this off," he said, placing one knee on the bed, right between her thighs.

Greedily, Nush scooted closer as he reached for the hem of her sleeveless tee. His laughter surrounded her as he realized what she'd been trying to do and he pulled her onto his thigh.

Nush threw her head back, clinging to him as his hard thigh gave her the friction she desperately wanted. She didn't know how he managed to get the tee off or when he'd climbed onto the bed and lifted her atop him until she was straddling him or when he'd got her panties off.

All she knew was that he gave her everything she needed. His calloused hands roaming her bare skin, cupping and kneading her breasts, his fingers drawing mindless circles around her nipples, and his thick erection nudging against the folds of her sex.

"Open your eyes, Nush. Look at me."

If he asked her to follow him the through the

gates of hell just then, Nush would've happily done so. The sight that met her eyes tightened the fist tugging down in her lower belly. He still had his jeans on even though the button was undone and her sex was indecently open and rubbing against the hard ridge of his abdomen, while his erection nudged at her buttocks.

Heat crested her cheeks at the wetness she'd left on his bare skin. As she watched, he rubbed the dampness onto his skin with one long, elegant finger, the act downright filthy and erotic. And then he brought the tip of his finger to his mouth and licked it away.

"How do I taste?" Nush asked, any nervousness she'd felt earlier misting away at the dark, hungry gleam in his eyes. It was liberating that she could say anything that came to her mind and he only found it arousing.

Hair mussed by her fingers, mouth swollen from her greedy kisses, he looked like the stuff of her wet fantasies come true. He gave a thoughtful hum, as if considering the question before he said, "Like you're mine."

Nush arched into his touch, her spine elongating like a cat stretching, desire vibrating through her body. And Caio played her perfectly.

Touching her everywhere but never lingering long enough.

Over and over, bringing her to the edge and talking her down.

Asking her to trust him when she protested.

Filthy curses flying from his own mouth when she dug her teeth into his shoulder, encouraging her to do to him as she pleased.

It was like waiting for a storm and yet not knowing when it would hit.

Tongue and teeth licking and tugging at her nipples, those clever fingers learning and re-learning her folds, his thumb playing decadent peekaboo with her clit, he pushed her toward the peak all over again. Soon, every inch of her was damp with sweat, muscles tense and tight, skin oversensitized.

She ground down on his fingers when he penetrated her, cursing at him to go faster when he barely moved them inside her, screaming that she hated him when he edged her once again, and then finally, he gave it to her with a gleaming smile and a whispered "You're achingly perfect and you're all mine, Princesa."

The orgasm caught her by surprise and ripped through her, stealing her breath, making her sob incoherently, while she chanted Caio's name like it was a benediction. She should've been used to it—to the physical and emotional cleansing it felt like every time he made her come.

Like he'd smashed her into pieces and put her

back together again and every time, she emerged a little different. A little less scared of her own heart.

It was minutes before Nush could form some kind of coherent thought. She was on her back, Caio's fingers lazily drifting up and down her side, her breaths still shallow and too fast. The cold of the damp sheets was a welcome contrast to the pockets of heat still tingling over her skin.

"I thought I died," she said, tasting salt on her tongue.

"I wouldn't let anything happen to you, Princesa." He asked, a sudden gravity to his tone, "You okay?"

"You know when I went on all those dates with all those men over the last year?" she said, her throat hoarse after all the moaning and sobbing, her words shooting out of a place she hadn't even known she wanted to visit. Especially in front of Caio.

Maybe the orgasm had undone not only her body but unlocked her heart too.

It's just damn good sex, Nushie, she could hear Yana say with a roll of her eyes. *Not magical healing.*

But neither could Nush discount the fact that this intimacy hadn't been possible for her with any other man except Caio, because she was emotionally invested in him already. Because she'd needed this real intimacy to go further.

The sudden tension that gripped Caio was a tangible thing in the air that plucked at Nush's wooly head. "Is this punishment for stringing your release along for too long?" His voice was only half joking.

But it didn't stop Nush. It seemed nothing could now.

"I was trying to get you out of my head. It got distressing to see you every day, every minute, to be so close and not tell you that I… I was determined that I'd prove to myself that it was just attraction. Lust. I'd idolized you for so long and somewhere along the line, it morphed into this… desire. I desperately wanted you to see me as a woman. I built up all these insecurities about why you didn't and I drove myself nuts."

"You're the most beautiful woman I've ever seen, Princesa."

To her pleasant surprise, Nush found that his words sank deep, that she believed him wholeheartedly. He saw beauty in her, conveyed it in his words, his touch, his kisses, and who was she to question that? All the ways he made her respond, the pleasure her body sang for him, what they had together was beautiful and powerful in itself. More than simple chemistry.

"Thank you," she said, running a finger over the furrow between his brows.

He held her wrist and again, pushed his face into her touch. "We don't have to talk about this. Now or ever."

And that sent a niggle through her. He was so reluctant to hear about her feelings for him, even as he demanded all that she had to give. "I'm not ashamed of how I feel, Caio. It's just that I think I see it finally. Why it didn't work with any of them. Why even when they were nice and pleasant, I couldn't go through with it. I used to think it was a mental block to do with how...everyone called me weird for so long."

His silence, instead of discouraging her, prodded her on.

"It was a block but not that. I simply didn't want any of those men even if I convinced myself I did. I've been in love with you for so long that...it was the last thing I wanted to admit to. I tried to purge it by going out with others. But my heart wasn't in it. And I backed off every time and my reputation grew even more bizarre."

As wrapped up as he was around her, Nush felt the tension that gripped him. What was heartfelt on her part gave way to an awkwardness she couldn't seem to dispel. Still, she tried. "That I love you...it's as natural as breathing for me, Caio. It's not a demand or a price or a weapon. It simply just is."

Caio kissed her shoulder, gathering her to him with tender reverence that plucked at her heart. "You're a gift I don't deserve, Nush."

And then he kissed her again, before she could argue with his questionable concept of deserving again, pushing her back into the sheets.

There was an urgency and something more to his kisses, a sense of determination. As if he wanted to make up for something he couldn't give.

The final piece of puzzle in place, Nush let herself float on the cloud of pleasure he pushed her onto. Already, all of her was addicted to him. And now she tested the words on her lips, of the truth she'd fought for so long.

She was in love with Caio. That was her truth. Her vulnerability. Her strength. And there wasn't much she could actually do about it. Her past and her present and her future all irrevocably tied to him who only dealt in absolutes. In words like *loyalty* and *commitment* and *deals.* In the past that was full of pain and ache and hatred.

She'd been in love with him for as long as she could remember. She wondered if she should be scared, if she should worry that he didn't feel the same but all her *shoulds* melted as he worshipped her with his mouth.

There wasn't an inch of her he didn't kiss, an inch of her he didn't learn. An inch of her he didn't bring into sharp clarity, teaching her new, exciting things about pleasure and her own body and how he could make her addicted to it all.

His hands were everywhere but stayed nowhere. Never long enough or lingering enough. On the bare swells of her breasts. Over one of her peaked nipples that was wet and glistening. Over her hips that bore his fingers' imprints. Over her thighs that she'd compulsively wrapped around his hips. Only inciting her further, only driving her toward that peak that she'd already thrown herself off.

He built her all over and all the while Nush was aware of the press of his thick, hard length against her outer thigh. "Can I touch you?"

His answer was a grin against her mouth before he drew her hand to his shaft and guided her fingers.

Turning on her side, unable to see him, Nush let touch and sensation speak to her. He was hard and thick and pulsing in her clasp. She traced the tip of it with her finger and found a drop of liquid. Her sex clenched, hungry for him all over again. Dampness fluttered even as her clit felt swollen and sensitive. "Is this okay?"

"Everything's okay between us, Nush," he

said, thrusting his hips into her clasp as she moved her fist up and down.

Releasing his erection, she brought her finger to her lips and tasted him. He was unlike anything she'd ever tasted and the dark gleam in his eyes made her want to lick him up all over. "I'm not ready to swallow yet, but that's my goal. Just so you know."

A filthy curse from him echoed around them. "I don't know whether to mar you or worship you."

"Why does it have to be one or the other?" she said, sending her hand on another foray. His shaft twitched in her hand, and the more she fisted it, the more Nush could see the tension vibrate through him. A displeased growl fell from her mouth as she could only do so much with one hand out of commission.

She fell onto her back and he followed, and finally, oh, finally, he bore down on her. Not giving her all of his weight though. Nush panted at the delicious weight of him and her thighs instantly fell open for him. Like a cat in heat, she rubbed her bare breasts against his hair-roughened chest and the erotic shock of that sensation made her roll her eyes back.

Nush nudged her hips upward, following instincts she didn't know she possessed and it was the most delicious feeling she'd ever known. And then he was there, running the head of his cock through her folds, drenching himself in her wetness, igniting a thousand sparks all over again.

"Hold on to me, Princesa."

Nush did, breaths coming helter-skelter now as the fat head of his erection dipped into her heat. It was tight and hot and her heart felt like it would beat out of her chest if he didn't continue.

"Look into my eyes, Nush. Keep touching me and yourself. Give me everything you've got, *minha esposa*."

Nush followed his order, melting at the gravelly command. Melting at the taste of him. Melting at the feel of his taut, tense muscles rippling as she raked her fingernails down his skin. Melting as sensations she'd never known before, pain and pleasure, suffused her.

Caio drove into her inch by merciless inch, going impossibly slow and she knew from the concrete set of his jaw that it was costing him every bit of his steely control.

Arching up, she rubbed herself against his chest. Touched him everywhere, whispering to him that she wanted all of him. And then with one merciless thrust, he penetrated her so deep that he was a part of her.

The pain was intense, cleaving through her pelvis, but fled as fast as it came. She gasped in air through her mouth, willing herself to breathe through it. Eyes closed, fingers digging into his shoulder, she tried not to betray her shaking. Not to give in to fear and push him off.

"I'm sorry, Nush," Caio breathed out. "Taking longer would only prolong the pain."

A drop of sweat hitting her shoulder made her look up. Golden eyes darkened impossibly, his jaw was so tight that a muscle jumped violently in his cheek. The regret in his eyes was like a balm to the pain that was already fleeting. Giving way to an achy fullness that she wanted to explore.

Nush clasped his cheek, pushed up and kissed him. Even the little movement made her gasp, her pelvic muscles clenching and releasing in an instinctive reaction. "I know," she said, rubbing her cheek against his like a cat.

"Don't, Anushka," he gritted out as a warning making her giggle. "Let me catch my breath."

His lips were soft and gentle, a sizzling contrast to the impossible hardness of him inside her. Wrapping her legs higher on his hips, Nush clung to him with one arm around his back. "It's almost gone, Caio."

He licked into her mouth with a groan. "That was the worst, Princesa. I'll make it better and better every time."

"I know." She stretched as he drew a line of kisses down her throat, wondering if it would ever stop feeling so new, so fervent. If she'd ever have enough of him. "Hey Caio?"

"Yes, Nush?"

"Do you think we can be ambitious enough to try and make me come again?"

He laughed, just as she'd intended and Nush fell in love with him all over again.

He was hers, irrevocably, and the simple fact terrorized her as much as it made her want to fly.

Her laughter and her wanton request were as arousing as the tight clutch of her sex. It had taken everything Caio had and more to be gentle when her wet heat had begun swallowing him with the same greediness that Nush showed in her words.

Sex was all he'd ever known but with Nush, it was making love, as much as he wanted to deny it. In this, he yielded the fight with grace.

This woman he'd married for all the wrong reasons demanded to be made love to, so he did it. Showing her with his mouth and fingers and his kisses and caresses that she was already invaluable to him. Making love to her because it was the only thing he could give her.

Not for a second did he forget the utter disbelief and horror in her eyes when he'd told her about his intentions for his father's company. If it could even be called that anymore.

But how could he stop now? How could he have any peace if he didn't see this through? How he could start a new chapter of his life with Nush if he didn't destroy the ugly pain and ache he'd stored up as if it were life-giving elixir?

If he didn't burn it all down and start afresh— the humiliation he'd suffered at Carlos's cruel taunts, the pain he'd suffered at his bullying son Enzo's fists, the agony of knowing that his mother had no strength to defy the man she'd married in haste, not even to protect Caio, the shattering of his heart when he realized she'd simply cast him out to protect her other sons, the loneliness, the pain of being ripped from the only home he'd ever known, of losing his father's legacy... He had to burn all the pain and bitterness away. Only then Nush could have what little was left of him fully, without those demons haunting him. Without the need for revenge hollowing him out. Only then could he break free and build a future she'd brought to shape.

She'd always known him as this hard shell of a man. She'd picked him, had chosen to tie her life with his, knowing this was all he could give her. She'd confessed her love for him, knowing he wouldn't return it, he reminded himself.

No, his path was made.

It was only her easy declaration that had

shaken him. That had planted all these doubts in his head.

"Caio?"

"Yes, *querida*?"

"Are you…is everything okay?"

He looked down and his heart ached at the picture she made. Wide eyes that demanded all his secrets, wavy hair spread out behind her, silky skin sweat dampened, mouth glistening pink… she was his every fantasy come true. "Yes. It's more than okay, Nush. You, me, this… It's better than I could've ever imagined."

She smiled then and it felt like basking in the warmth of a sun after a long, dark winter. "It doesn't hurt that much anymore. Can you…? Can we…?" She gave an experimental thrust of her hips and fire rippled down his spine, pooling low.

He groaned, licked the drop of sweat dripping down the valley between her breasts.

Pushing away any other doubts that threatened to mar the sheer bliss of this moment for her and him, he kissed her gently.

Just a few more days and he would be…ready for this. Fully ready. Fully free.

Amassing all the patience and reverence and his experience, he applied himself to giving her the one thing she had asked of him.

Holding himself off her on one elbow, he

plucked at the taut nipple calling for his attention. He licked it, before sucking into his mouth and beneath him, Nush trembled, arching off the bed into him. Demanding more.

More, more and more, even as if he gave her everything.

Even as she clung to his neck with one arm, she sent her other hand on a quest of his body. Fingers like butterfly wings explored his neck, his pecs, his abdomen, and Cristo, where they were joined even.

The woman was analytical and there was no stopping her curiosity.

A growl escaped his mouth as he felt her fingers flutter over his balls, traced over the root of his cock, following to the folds of her sex. "Touch your clit, Nush."

"Yes sir," she whispered cheekily and drew circles over her clit. Seeing her fingers move over that swollen flesh, Cristo, that was an image that would haunt him forever.

He pulled out, and thrust in, a deep heat gathering at the base of his spine.

Her own growl joined his. "I'm getting there, Caio. God, please push me off. Now."

Lifting her hips off the bed, he thrust in and out at an angle, his own climax reaching and roaring for him.

"Oh…" she whispered, head thrown back as

he hit her clit on the way in and out. "Caio, I feel it. I feel it here," she said, touching the slit of her sex when he'd almost pulled out completely.

He grinned and their eyes met. "Collecting all the data, Princesa?"

"You know it." Sweat-dampened brow, lush full lips, and chest covered in his stubble burn, she was the most erotic thing he'd ever seen. "Now, harder. Caio. Please, faster."

"Keep touching yourself," he whispered and then his rhythm became something else.

It became madness. It became a hungry bellow from his chest. It became a hungry claiming like he'd never known before.

She got her wish, screaming out his name as she climaxed and her clenching muscles tipped Caio over. He came with a hard burning rasp wrenched from his throat, heat invading every limb and muscle and leaving him shaken. For a few seconds, he allowed himself the luxury of feeling her under him, burying his face in her neck and inhaling the scent their bodies coated the air with. In his arms, she felt small, fragile and yet there was such power in her to…shatter him if she wished.

The thought made his chest cold and he moved to lift away from her.

Her hands on his shoulder, she stopped him.

"We did it," Nush whispered, eyes gleaming, and his heart thumped unsteadily in his chest.

Suddenly, his life without Nush in it didn't bear thinking about. Maybe this wasn't something he'd imagined his life to play out, but he wasn't foolish enough to reject a gift just because he hadn't recognized it immediately for what it was. But would her love for him last when he didn't return it? When it would always be marred by a shadow of disbelief and fear that she'd take it back?

Would she realize one day that he didn't deserve it?

CHAPTER TWELVE

IT WAS LUNCHTIME when Caio jumped out of the helicopter and signaled his pilot to leave. He'd been terse and short and unsettled all day and most of his team had sighed out in relief when he'd announced that he was taking off for the day.

As the chopper's wind blew at him, playing with his hair and clothes, Caio admitted the truth he'd been fighting all week.

His heart was not in it anymore. In seeing his plans through—the very plans it had taken him more than a decade to set in motion.

Seeing his stepfather Carlos's face turn frightfully purple as Caio had walked into his office two days ago to reveal to him that he was the designer of his destruction had not been as satisfactory as he'd expected. Not when he had to face the diseased spirit of employees who had been with the company from his father's time.

The last decade and more had not been kind

to Carlos. In fact, Caio wondered if his ruin had begun from the day Caio's mother had died.

It had only left him with disgust as to how many lives Carlos had actually ruined. And neither had there been satisfaction in seeing his stepbrother Enzo dragged away by the police for embezzling pension funds, for all the Ponzi schemes he'd run using Caio's father's name. Not when Caio had also been witness to Enzo's wife's tears—a woman Caio himself had once liked. In the battle that had resulted between him and Enzo, Sophia had chosen Enzo, knowing of Caio's imminent ruin, and expulsion from his own father's company.

But nothing in him today had liked the misery on Sophia's face or seeing the framed picture of her three kids on her desk whose futures had been shattered by everything Caio had unleashed.

All he had known then was that he had to leave. Nothing was going as he'd planned. It hadn't felt like freedom from the fury that had coursed through him, corroding him for years. It hadn't felt like relief from the isolation he'd felt, from his family, from his own identity as the son who'd been loved by his parents.

He'd thought he'd feel redeemed, different, maybe even renewed.

But all he'd felt was…this gnawing, aching

sense of loss. This emptiness, as if revenge had scoured him and left him with nothing.

Only the thought of returning to Nush had energized him.

He needed to see Nush, needed to touch her and hold her. He needed to make sure she was still there, to reassure himself that she was the only certainty left in his life.

He heard the laughter long before he saw them, as he walked around the house. They were sitting at a table next to the pool, heads bent together, and laughing. The woman was Anushka, Caio knew that. He would know that laughter anywhere.

Finally, he could see them.

She was dressed in a pink top that dangled off her shoulder, and black shorts with her legs kicked out. The man…his profile seemed familiar. Even as Caio frowned, the man pointed to something, Nush laughed and swatted him on the shoulder.

Another step, another hard breath and Caio knew.

He knew who the man was.

As if punched by an invisible first in his gut, every inch of him stilled. It was a wonder he hadn't put up his fists to defend himself. That was how painfully real that hit felt.

Thoughts and questions swirled through him, like lines in a complex algorithm that flashed across the screen when the program he and Nash built together ran. He couldn't pin anything down. He even made a half turning motion, some primitive instinct part of him urging him to flee.

It felt like betrayal—her sitting with him. Her talking with him. Her laughter with his brother. Her going behind his back.

"Caio? You're back."

Caio hadn't seen Javier since he had arrived in Brazil. If he was completely honest with himself, he'd been avoiding Javier.

Even though Javi had called his assistant several times, requesting a meeting. He'd even showed up once outside of Caio's temporary HQ but he'd pretended to have not seen the younger man. Just like he hadn't set foot in the headquarters of his father's company.

It wasn't Carlos or Enzo or his other brother Jorge that he had wanted to avoid. But this young man in front of him, who reminded Caio the most of their mother.

Caio watched him now with the greediness, all the limits and restrictions placed on himself blown to smithereens by his conniving little wife. It was another punch to his gut—how much Javier looked like Caio himself.

He counted to some arbitrary number before he let his gaze touch Anushka.

As if aware of this microaggression, she raised her brows and glared at him, instead of looking even remotely guilty.

He let her see his fury.

She sighed, her large eyes drinking him in greedily. "If you have something to say, Caio, please feel free to do it."

"We will deal with our...issues in privacy, *minha esposa*," he said, enunciating the endearment. He was blazingly angry and yet the anger seemed to wash away resentment and the sense of betrayal that he wanted to hold on to. Because anything he felt around the blasted woman was far too real and welcome. Even his body seemed to know that but not his rational mind. "After I deal with the unwanted guest."

"Caio, I apologize—" his brother began.

Hand on his shoulder, Nush defended Javi as if he were her cub. "No, Javi. Don't apologize," she said, standing up. "This is not just his house. It's mine too. My home. And as such, I'm allowed to have guests. If Caio doesn't like that, then he can go inside and take his black mood with him."

Caio couldn't remember another occasion— not even as a boy—when someone had so outrageously provoked his temper. Not only had she gone behind his back and invited his brother here, but now she dared to defend Javi, to throw herself in front of him as if Caio would eat him alive…

"What the hell are you smiling at, Javier?" The question burst out of him before he had consciously decided that he would speak to his brother. A part of him wanted to dismiss him, have him thrown out of this house, this new life he was building for himself. A part of him wanted not even the shadow of his brother to touch Anushka. But clearly, it was too late for that.

The diplomat he always was, Javi just shrugged. "Congratulations on your wedding, Caio. Your wife is…" His mouth twitching, he cast Nush a sideways glance, and even in just the flash of a second, Caio could see how smitten Javier was with her, and he had to swallow down an irrational spurt of jealousy. "She is delightful," Javier finished. "I'm glad to see you settled and happy, finally." There was such genuine emotion in Javi's words that Caio's own anger ebbed as fast as it had come. And he wasn't ready for that.

"I've been happy for a long time, Javi," he added, like a petulant schoolboy. Even though he knew his words were false.

"Can you really say that?" Javier demanded in a soft voice. "Because if you've been so happy, why have you been hiding from me? Why carry out your elaborate charade of stripping everything from Carlos but avoid me and Jorge?"

"Get out," Caio said finally in a soft whisper.

"No," Nush said, defiance shining in her gaze. "Not until you listen to what he has to say. Please, Caio… I went to a lot of trouble to get him here."

"I told you it was useless, Anushka," Javi said, his eyes on Caio. "He has turned his back on us a long time ago. It is only you who holds impossible dreams and hopes for him."

Ire flared in Caio's depths. "Don't talk to my wife like that."

"Why not? The foolish woman thinks the world of you when you can't even——"

When Caio would've punched him in the face, Nush stopped him with a hand on his chest. "Jesus, Caio. Can't you see that he's provoking you?" She pressed her forehead into his chest, wrapping her arms around him. "Just give him a chance."

"You shouldn't have interfered, Princesa. This is none of your business," he said, tucking his hands into his pockets and turning away from her. He closed his eyes when he heard her soft gasp. And he had to stiffen himself, stop himself from soothing the hurt.

"Everything that concerns you is my business. This path of destruction you're on is my business."

He turned toward her, feeling like a cornered, wounded animal. "Walk away if I'm not good enough for you, Nush. But please, don't assume to know my pain."

Nush flinched, and still, she didn't walk away. "You don't mean that?"

"Whatever you think this will do, you're wrong," he said, gentling his words. "I have had more than a decade to nurse this resentment and anger and pain. Nothing Javier tells me today is going to get rid of it."

Clasping his face with her hands, Nush pressed a soft kiss to his lips. "This is not a quid pro quo. My promise to you is unconditional. But I can't see you ripping yourself in half either. Please, Caio, do this for me. I've never asked you for anything before."

She walked away, leaving him feeling alone in the entire world all over again.

Hands tucked into his pockets, Caio turned to his brother. "What's there for us to discuss, Javi? What can you feel for me after I've destroyed your father and brother? Because I won't take that back for anyone. Carlos and Enzo deserve to rot in jail."

His brother scowled. "You think I'm here to beg for mercy on their behalf?"

"Or to curse me for ruining them?"

"I know you have had a long time to hate all of us, Caio. And I can't even blame you for any of it. It took me and Jorge a long time to see Papa's true nature. It took me a long time to catch up to how Enzo was bullying Jorge right under my nose. The same thing he did to you…"

A feral sound escaped Caio's mouth but it wasn't because of the past. It was at the thought of their gentle, quiet, artistic brother Jorge being Enzo's new victim. He rubbed a hand over his face and found it shaking. "Enzo bullied Jorge?"

Javi nodded after a hard swallow. "I did my best to stop him, to remove Jorge from his presence. I used all the money you kept sending us to protect Jorge."

"Why didn't you just leave?" Caio thundered, guilt a fresh thorn under his skin.

For so long, he hadn't even looked back and now, to realize that he could have put an end to all this, that he could've stopped Jorge from being hurt as he had been once.

"You never once looked back," Javi said, pain and even resentment etched into his own face. "You just left one day, Caio. Without goodbye.

Without uttering a word to me or Jorge. And then Mama fell sick. I looked after her while she pined over you. She died of a broken heart, Caio. And all the time, Enzo and Papa kept telling me and Jorge lies about you. Who do you think I'd believe first?"

Caio closed his eyes, a part of him shying away from meeting his brother's gaze. "I sent you money."

"And that was the first sign that you even cared about us, the first communication I had from you after years." A bitter laugh escaped his brother's throat. "We needed you, Caio. Not your money. When Anushka called," he said, casting a glance in the direction of the house, "I grabbed the chance to come see you. Jorge didn't want to but I did."

"It's too late to save them, Javi—"

"You think I couldn't have told Papa that it was you who was masterminding the whole thing from behind the scenes?" Javi shook his head. "I haven't come here to ask you for anything, Caio. Not for me, not for Jorge, not for Papa. I came to tell you that Mama loved you. That she thought of you every minute, every day after you left. That it broke her heart that she had to let you go."

"She had a choice, she could have—"

"She had me and Jorge to look after. You think

Papa would have let us go with her? Can't you see this from her point of you, Caio? She did her best by us and by you. Did you know that she called Rao and begged him to give you a new direction?"

Caio felt as if someone had delivered another punch. "She asked Rao?"

Javier nodded. "When he did his monthly checkup, yes. She knew the best thing for you was to leave that toxic environment." His brother sighed. "I...thought you should know. Jorge and I are your brothers, your family. She'd have wanted me to take this step. She'd have..."

His brother broke off, overwhelmed with emotion and left without another word.

Caio stayed by the pool long after darkness swallowed his shadows, wondering at how much his revenge had robbed from him. How much he had willingly lost. How many years he could have had with two brothers.

And he had hurt the one woman who'd cared enough to help him see the truth, despite his bullheadedness.

When Caio returned to the house, a tightness in his chest that he couldn't swallow past, the living room and the kitchen greeted him with silence. He made his way to the bedroom to find Nash methodically packing her new clothes into a bag on the bed. Fear crawled through him like spider legs skittering all over, fisting his chest in a vise grip.

"What are you doing?" he demanded with his usual arrogance.

"Yana's agent called me. She fainted yesterday during a shoot. Mira, as you know, has just returned to Aristos. I want to spend a few days looking after Yana. You know she's not that great with managing her type one diabetes."

"I thought you would at least tell me the truth instead of using what seems to be the perfect excuse."

Nush whirled to face him. "Perfect excuse for what?"

"To leave me. What else?" Caio didn't think he had ever felt as hollow and empty as he did then.

"Leave you?" Nush said, her brow tying into that frown that he loved to kiss. Arms folded, she considered from beneath those thick glasses, her hair in a messy knot he wanted to unravel. "You think I'm leaving you?"

"You were right. I set up my stepfather using his own greed to fall. I used all the information I had against Enzo to get him behind bars. For more than fifteen years, all I tried to do was to pay them back for what they took from me."

Nush stared at him as if she had never seen

him before. He wondered if he would see disgust in her expression finally. "Did it feel good?"

It was the last question he had expected and he had no self-preservation left to hide it from himself or her. He sat down on the bed next to the suitcase, leaving enough distance between them so that she didn't have to step back if she didn't want him near her. "No." He thrust his fingers through his hair. "I've been struggling with it for weeks, waiting for it to feel good. Then, I was waiting for it to feel less horrible, less dirty. I thought bringing them down, showing them what I had made of myself, how powerful and wealthy I was..." he couldn't help the laugh that escaped his mouth, "would take away the pain and loss I felt all those years ago. I thought destroying them would help me gain something of myself back. Instead, it felt like it was tainting me too, all the innocent lives I was walking away from, in ruins. It was their fate with Carlos, sooner or later, but still... In the last day, I've been wondering if you were right. If I should be saving the company instead. If I should save things instead of ruining them."

She didn't say anything for a long time and Caio wondered if there was nothing left to say. She mirrored his pose and sat down on the bed leaving the bag between them. It felt like an ocean between them, taunting him, mocking him for everything he'd failed.

"I know it was sneaky to go behind your back and find Javier but I had to," she said finally. "The more I dug about your father's company, your stepbrother's embezzlement, all the shady deals Carlos has been making...it dawned on me what you meant to do. I could see it in your eyes, Caio, what it was costing you. And then of course my curiosity wouldn't stop there. I found Javier and called him. I don't know what I was thinking I'd do if he turned out to be like your stepbrother. But I had to take the chance."

"A chance on what, Princesa?"

"A chance that you might gain a brother or two back, Caio. A chance for you to have a family again. You brought me to mine when I was struggling. You helped me make right decisions for Mama. You were my strength, my rock when Thaata and Nanamma died. Why wouldn't I want to do the same for you?"

Caio scoffed. "Are you saving me, Nush? Because I've lived with this rage for so long that I don't know what I would be without it, Princesa."

She scoffed back. "Save you? You think this is some debt that I'm paying? I told you I love you, Caio. To see you unhappy, to see you miserable and angry, to see you hate yourself...it hurts me. What kind of a life would you and I have if this path of destruction you've been on destroyed you too?" She shook her head. "This was purely selfish. I want a future with you. I want to have kids with you. I want my kids to have a father who loves them with his whole heart. I did this all for myself. For my future."

Throwing the bag between them down on the floor, Caio rolled Nush underneath him on the bed. "Letting go of all that poison, all that hatred after all these years…it's terrifying. I'm afraid that there will be nothing left in me. That it has eaten away at anything good and whole."

She pushed his hair off his forehead, her big eyes stinging with gentle strength. "You already know that's not true. That's why Thaata wanted to stop you too. You're your father's son, Caio. You're Rao's protégé. You're my fairy-tale knight. You're the big brother Yana's always wanted. You're the steadfast friend Mira said she'd always needed. You couldn't be all these things to all of us if there was nothing good in you. There's a reason you've been fighting yourself the last two weeks. A reason this was eating away at you."

"Then you're my saving grace, Princesa."

Pushing up on her elbows, she leaned her forehead against his, her cheeks damp with tears. "No. You just needed a nudge. You… I love you so much, Caio, that it terrifies me every day. I trust your word that you wouldn't abandon me but I wanted to do it because you love me, because you need me as much as I—" A sob burst through her words.

"Shh… Princesa. No tears. I'd hate myself if I made you cry."

"I thought I could stick it out, be happy with what you give me, but I can't." Her open eyes held his. "I want it all, Caio. I can't—"

Pressing his face into her throat, Caio said the words that had been battling to be let out of his chest for quite a while now. "I don't know what I did to deserve you…but don't walk away now, *Princesa*. I want that future you're promising me. I want to be the husband you deserve. I want our kids to be surrounded by aunts and uncles like I was once. I can't imagine a single day without you in my life, Nush. I'll spend the rest my life proving to you how much I love you. How much I need you."

Her hand in his hair tugged his head up and he saw that his clever wife hadn't missed anything. "You'll reconcile with Javier and Jorge?"

He nodded, swallowing the tears that had hardened in his throat. "Yes. Javier made me face some choice truths I was too angry and hurt to see. He told me that Mama was the one who asked Rao to take me away."

Joy bloomed through Nush's chest at the thread of hope in Caio's eyes. "She did?"

"It was the only choice left to her. Carlos would've taken Jorge and Javier from her if she even tried to…so she made sure I got out of there. And she…"

Hand in his hair, Nush held him as Caio buried his face in her chest, his big, broad shoulders trembling. Mouth at his temple, she kissed him and calmed him and whispered all the things she could.

"I'm so sorry you never got to see her again, Caio. I can't…" Her own tears beckoned. "But she loved you. And all the anger and rage and pain…it hasn't tainted you, Caio. It's hardened you. It's…"

He looked up then. "You think there's hope for me then, *querida*?"

"Hope, Caio? You're my hero, my knight, my everything. I'd have never fallen in love with a man who found pleasure in hurting others. You and I both know you were already struggling with this. I just wish…"

"That's because of you and Rao and Mira and Yana and all the love you showed me. If you hadn't proposed our wedding—" A shudder went through him and Nush giggled.

"Laughing at my pain, Princesa? That's a cheap shot."

Any sweet words she wanted to offer evaporated when Caio shifted on top of her completely and proceeded to punish her with hard, demanding kisses. "I love you, Caio," she whispered, her heart and body both soaring.

"I love you, *minha esposa*. And if you need to visit Yana, I understand."

"A part of me doesn't want to leave you so soon. I'm afraid that—"

"No more than five days, Princesa. You can't be her keeper. Not when you have a husband you have to keep on the straight and narrow."

Nush giggled then. "What will you do?"

"I have a lot of reparations to make. Starting with convincing my brothers that I want to be a part of their life. And then, when you are back, you and I will make a plan to rebuild my father's company."

"Then we better get busy then."

"With what, Nush?"

"We need to have five days' worth of sex before I leave. Or else I might go into withdrawal."

His hands were moving before Nush had finished talking. She gasped as those fingers began weaving their magic as Caio whispered, "Fast or slow, Princesa?"

"Hard first and then slow," Nush whispered, taking his mouth in a rough kiss.

Her heart stuttered with joy as Caio drove her body all the way to the peak again.

* * * * *

Couldn't stop turning the pages of
Marriage Bargain with Her Brazilian Boss?
Don't miss the next installment in the
Billion-Dollar Fairy Tales trilogy,
coming soon!

In the meantime, catch these other stories
by Tara Pammi!

Claiming His Bollywood Cinderella
The Surprise Bollywood Baby
The Playboy's "I Do" Deal
Returning for His Unknown Son
The Secret She Kept in Bollywood

Available now!

Tara Pammi can't remember a moment when she wasn't lost in a book—especially a romance, which was much more exciting than a mathematics textbook at school. Years later, Tara's wild imagination and love for the written word revealed what she really wanted to do. Now she pairs alpha males who think they know everything with strong women who knock that theory and them off their feet!

Books by Tara Pammi

Harlequin Presents

Returning for His Unknown Son

Born into Bollywood

Claiming His Bollywood Cinderella
The Surprise Bollywood Baby
The Secret She Kept in Bollywood

Once Upon a Temptation

The Flaw in His Marriage Plan

Signed, Sealed...Seduced

The Playboy's "I Do" Deal

Visit the Author Profile page
at Harlequin.com for more titles.